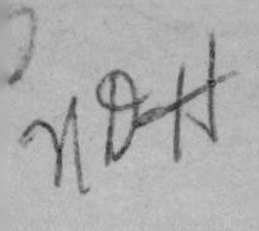

"What's so frightening about being happy?"

Leith spoke softly, his fingers gently trailing over her cheek.

"Oh, Leith." Carolyn gulped. "There are things about me you—you don't know." Fear clutched at her, telling her to enjoy her happiness for as long as it lasted.

"I think I already know your dreadful secret," Leith said quietly. "I'd say you weren't married when you had your son. Am I right?"

Carolyn nodded slowly, too stunned to speak. "Do you think that could possibly make any difference to the way I feel about you?" he asked huskily.

Tears burned behind her eyes as guilt assailed her. Tell him all of it, she told herself. "Oh, Leith—hold me," she whispered desperately, and his arms tightened around her.

LYNSEY STEVENS, an Australian author, has a sense of humor that adds a lively quality to her writing. While enjoying her work as a librarian, her first love is writing. In addition to her Presents novels she has also written historical romance, adventure and espionage. Though her first romance novel was rejected, Lynsey now has several published books to her credit. And she hints at the presence of a real live Harlequin hero in her life!

Books by Lynsey Stevens

HARLEQUIN PRESENTS

497—RYAN'S RETURN
606—MAN OF VENGEANCE
654—FORBIDDEN WINE
692—STARTING OVER
774—LINGERING EMBERS

HARLEQUIN ROMANCE

2488—PLAY OUR SONG AGAIN
2495—RACE FOR REVENGE
2507—TROPICAL KNIGHT
2574—CLOSEST PLACE TO HEAVEN
2608—THE ASHBY AFFAIR
2706—TEREBORI'S GOLD

LYNSEY STEVENS

leave yesterday behind

Harlequin Books

TORONTO • NEW YORK • LONDON
AMSTERDAM • PARIS • SYDNEY • HAMBURG
STOCKHOLM • ATHENS • TOKYO • MILAN

Harlequin Presents first edition July 1987
ISBN 0-373-10996-2

Original hardcover edition published in 1986
by Mills & Boon Limited

Printed in U.S.A.

CHAPTER ONE

CAROLYN hurried into her office and leant across to switch on the intercom. 'Morning, Mr Kruger,' she said brightly. 'Sorry I'm a little late. Car trouble again, I'm afraid.'

'Can you come right in, Carolyn?' Her boss's voice cut into the quietness of the room.

'Of course.' She frowned as she straightened. Did Mr Kruger sound a little flustered? He wouldn't be angry with her for being late because she'd worked late for an hour and a half the evening before so that they would be sure everything was in order. Yet he had sounded quite unlike himself. What could be wrong now? Not a hitch with the amalgamation, surely? Not today, when the representative from the other company was due to arrive.

On her way up in the lift she had run into Trevor Green, Kruger's accountant, and although he had laughed about what he had called the Southern Cavalry sending one of its generals to look over the new troops he had been quite serious about the financial state of Kruger's and just how much John Kruger was depending on this amalgamation.

Picking up her notepad and pencil she crossed to the connecting door that led into her boss's office. She tapped lightly and her hand was reaching out for the doorknob when the door was swung inwards and she was facing a tall grey-suited body, her gaze rising, startled, to meet a pair of piercingly bright blue eyes.

Those eyes held hers for a split second before she blinked and the rest of the man's features registered in her mind. The blood left her face and she clutched blindly for the door frame to steady herself. Involuntarily she took a shaky step backwards, away from him, and her notepad and pencil slipped through her nerveless fingers.

It couldn't be him! It couldn't! Fate wouldn't be so heartless. That chapter of her life was closed, locked tightly away. She hadn't forgotten, she never would be able to forget, but the last thing she wanted or needed was to be reminded. To see this particular man standing in front of her slashed open that old wound with one bitter effortless stroke.

He had changed. He seemed taller and broader and, of course, he was older. They both were—nearly fourteen years older, she thought hysterically. She had a momentary flash of him as he'd been then. Long, lean, dark and so very self-assured, even at twenty-two. And so savagely scathing. What was he doing here?

Carolyn couldn't tear her eyes from his face and she knew she wasn't disguising the shock and horror that reached down to her very soul. A frown of concern furrowed his brow and he made to move towards her.

Carolyn gasped and stumbled backwards again, letting go of the door frame, swaying on legs too unsteady to take her weight.

The room and the man in front of her spun crazily, and when everything righted itself she was stretched out on the leather-covered couch in Mr Kruger's office. Her boss was leaning worriedly over her, awkwardly patting her hand.

'Dear, dear,' he muttered concernedly, his glasses slipping down on his nose.

Foolishly Carolyn thought this was funny and she swallowed a chuckle, very afraid once she began to laugh she would be unable to stop. She struggled to sit upright.

'I'm sorry, Mr Kruger. I don't know——' She gulped convulsively as that same face appeared again.

He was back, real, not part of some horrendous nightmare, and this time he thrust one of Mr Kruger's crystal tumblers towards her. The glass shook and his hands, long, tanned and competent, covered hers to steady the glass, helping her guide it to her lips. The brandy ran fire down her throat and she coughed.

'Drink some more.' He spoke for the first time and his voice was deep and authoritative, matching his looks. Rugged. Masculine. And handsome—undeniably handsome. Even in the shock of the situation she registered that fact.

Carolyn took another sip, more cautiously this time, and the liquid began to warm her, bringing colour back into her cheeks. She took a deep breath and he released her hands, taking the glass from her.

'I'm sorry,' she repeated. 'I didn't expect . . . you gave me a fright.' She swung her legs on to the floor and gingerly stood up. What could she say? I didn't expect to see you again. Not ever.

She nervously patted her hair, soft fair hair pulled almost severely back into a chignon that emphasised the smooth curve of her jaw, her small pointed chin.

Her smoky-grey eyes were drawn back to him as she

waited for him to comment, to make some sign that he remembered, too. But he didn't. There was no shadow of recognition in those cold eyes, no suggestion he knew her.

But then, she thought bitterly, why should he? What was there left in her of the angry, confused, shocked and terribly frightened sixteen-year-old she had been all those years ago?

'You gave us quite a turn, young lady. Didn't she, Leith?' Mr Kruger commented as he shuffled around his desk to take his seat.

Carolyn noticed then that the older man looked a little drawn and haggard. He suffered from general ill-health and had his only son taken more interest in the business Carolyn was sure he would have retired a couple of years ago.

John Kruger chuckled. 'However, I'm sure you're used to young women falling at your feet, Leith.'

'No, I can't say I am. This was a totally new experience for me,' the other man said. 'But I have to admit, women don't usually go all pale at the sight of me.' He turned slightly and smiled easily at Carolyn. His amusement completely changed his face, running deep clefts in his cheeks, relaxing the stern line of his mouth, and his blue eyes sparkled making him look younger and so very much more potently attractive.

And Carolyn was totally aware she was not immune to that persuasive magnetism. The knowledge of her susceptibility shocked her almost as much as seeing him again had horrified her. Men, in the romantic sense, had no part in her life. She wanted it that way and she made very sure she kept it that way. It hadn't been difficult to do, to keep herself apart from everyone. Except Bodie. Bodie was the exception to the rule. He made her whole life worthwhile and she loved him more than she had ever imagined it was possible for her to love another human being.

But now this man, in mere moments, had turned her

whole carefully protected world inside out. He was the catalyst that set off the return of an agony of fear she had thought she'd never again have to experience. Hadn't she closed and locked that particular door on everything to do with that part of her life?

The devastating smile on his lips faded just slightly and Carolyn drew herself together with no small effort, knowing he had sensed her antipathy.

'Oh, no, it wasn't that,' she heard herself stammer. 'I wasn't expecting the door to open so suddenly and you . . . you startled me,' she finished lamely.

'What Carolyn means is I move a little more slowly these days,' John Kruger laughed. 'Anyway, let me introduce you two. Leith, this is Mrs Carolyn Allerton, the best secretary I've ever had. Carolyn, meet Leith McCabe from National Consolidated, or should I say, Mr NatCon, the boss of the whole outfit. NatCon will be taking over Kruger's.'

Leith McCabe was the southern general Trevor had been joking about. Leith McCabe? It was incredible. Impossible. Her mind clutched eagerly for straws. Perhaps he was just here to—to what? See all was in order. But anyone could have done that. He would have any number of employees he could have sent. It didn't need the biggest gun of all to check out Kruger's. Compared to the internationally known NatCon, Kruger's Construction was a puny pebble in a very large pond.

'Mrs Allerton.' He inclined his dark head. Had he paused slightly over the 'Mrs'?

Did she imagine his glance sliding to, and then away from the absence of a wedding-ring on her left hand? No! She was becoming paranoid.

Her eyes flicked towards Mr Kruger and fear clutched at her stomach, twisting unmercifully. There resting on his desk were the distinctively coloured folders holding the personnel files. And her own name sprang off the folder on top of the pile.

No! Don't panic! She made herself remain calm. What could he possibly learn from that file? Her mind flashed to the form she'd filled out eight years ago, when the burden of guilt still weighed heavily upon her. Allerton, Carolyn Leigh. Her date of birth. Marital Status: Widow. Next-of-kin: Josephine Brown, Aunt. What could all that tell him? Almost nothing. But not all truth, she reminded herself guiltily.

'How do you do,' she got out huskily, her body numb, her mind now spinning crazily as she tried to take in the implications of the whole dreadful situation.

'Leith will be working with me for a while to get everything into line with National Consolidated before I retire.'

John Kruger's words snatched Carolyn's full attention. 'Retire?' she repeated, her eyes swinging in surprise to her boss. 'But I—you didn't——'

'I know.' John Kruger held up his hand. 'I didn't say anything, not anything specific, about retiring, but I've had it in my mind for some time. Now that we've amalgamated,' he gave Leith McCabe a rueful grimace, 'with NatCon it seemed like as good a time as any. I feel confident about handing everything over to Leith and I know he'll do the right thing by our staff. So,' he leant back in his chair, 'Molly and I will be heading down to the coast at last for the well-earned rest we've been promising ourselves.'

Carolyn's mind was in a turmoil as she fought to disguise her dismay. Did this mean her job was in jeopardy? Surely not. She would be reassigned. Her heart plummeted. She had a wonderful working relationship with Mr Kruger, he was sympathetic of their circumstances, hers and Bodie's, and it would be difficult adjusting to someone else.

'When did you plan on leaving?' she asked him flatly, avoiding Leith McCabe's piercing gaze that seemed to see too much.

'Possibly two weeks. Perhaps sooner,' her boss replied,

and Carolyn gasped.

'Two weeks! But——'

John Kruger chuckled. 'You sound as though you'll be sorry to see me go, Carolyn!'

'You know I will, Mr Kruger. I've enjoyed working with you,' she said sincerely, and swallowed painfully. It was all a dreadful nightmare. It had to be.

'Carolyn's been with us for about, what, eight years now and she's been my secretary for the last seven, so she's coming well recommended,' he told Leith McCabe. 'You won't find a better secretary in Brisbane.'

A fearful tightness clutched at Carolyn's stomach as she slowly turned to look at Leith McCabe.

'Leith will need a good right hand here in Brisbane during the takeover,' John Kruger continued, 'and as you know almost as much about the workings of the firm as I do he feels you would be the best choice. I heartily agree with him.'

Carolyn's lips tightened and a light flush touched her cheeks. She was stiff with tension. How could she stay here and work with Leith McCabe? Her whole secure world was teetering dangerously on the brink of disaster.

So he hadn't as yet recognised her, but he wasn't a fool. It wouldn't take him long, surely, to see in her the girl he had every reason to hate. Working close to him would be like walking a daily tightrope waiting for the moment when something triggered his memory and he realised Carolyn Allerton and Carol Barton were one and the same.

Their conversation outside that Melbourne courtroom all those years ago was burned indelibly on her memory and she couldn't imagine he could possibly forget his merciless condemnation of her. She was unable to suppress an involuntary shiver and she saw the sudden narrowing of his eyes, all humour leaving their blue depths.

'If you have no objections,' his deep voice said evenly, with just a hint of dryness.

With a great deal of application Carolyn drew her shattered composure into some order. She needed her job badly, if only until she could find another one.

'No, of course not,'she said quickly, although she couldn't hold Leith McCabe's gaze.

'Fine.' John Kruger clasped his hands together. 'Well, I've dictated a memo to the rest of the staff putting them in the picture so perhaps you could get that on the road, Carolyn. By then we should be able to let you know how we're going to organise the office end of it.'

'Of course.' Carolyn walked towards the door to her own office, but Leith McCabe was there before her.

'By the way, what was wrong with your car?' John Kruger asked, and she paused, half turning back towards him.

'A flat tyre. It took me some time to change it,' she said, feeling the other man's proximity with what seemed like every sensitive nerve in her body.

'Dear me!' Mr Kruger tut-tutted. 'No muscular good Samaritan nearby to help you out?'

She smiled faintly. 'No, unfortunately not. My neighbours had all left for work.'

'You seem to be plagued by car trouble lately,' John Kruger continued conversationally while Carolyn screamed silently to be allowed to leave the room. And Leith McCabe. 'Perhaps you should think about trading it in for a more reliable one.'

'Yes,' Carolyn agreed. That was what she should do, but a new car was definitely outside their strict budget. She turned back to the doorway where Leith McCabe waited. 'Thank you,' she murmured huskily as she passed him, her whole body taut with a tension she was sure he couldn't fail to sense. It seemed to be emanating from her in ever-increasing waves.

'Mrs Allerton.' His deep voice caught her in midstride and she paused, turning slowly. With a mocking smile he handed her her notepad and pencil. She took them from him and fled.

Only when the door closed behind her did she expel the breath she was holding and sag back against the cool panel like a rag doll. It was some minutes before she found the strength to straighten and cross to her desk. She subsided into her chair, threw down the notepad and pencil and covered her face with her hands.

What was she going to do? How could he come back into her life? Surely she'd paid in full for her part in the tragedy? She'd suffered agonies of guilt over it, she still woke at night in a fever of despair, and she suspected she always would. That fragment of her life had been like riding a roller-coaster on a path to self-destruction. It had taken Bodie to save her.

Now to have Leith McCabe reappear with such inconceivable suddenness was as effective as a blow to the solar plexus. And it was especially brutal because she had begun to feel she had escaped, had travelled far enough away, had managed to lose herself in the anonymity of another city. But apparently she hadn't escaped at all, and now after fourteen long years it seemed she never would. Fate had been waiting to cut her down again and the folly of her recalcitrant youth was going to follow her wherever she went for the rest of her life.

And Bodie, what would it do to him, especially at this crucial stage? How would he cope with a major upheaval in their routine? And far worse, with finding out the complete truth? She'd have to tell him now, try to explain, just in case . . . Her heart ached for the relatively uncomplicated existence that was yesterday.

Slowly Carolyn began to pull herself together. There was no time to mull it over now. She had a job to do and she was going to do it. Arriving late wouldn't have made the best impression on the new general and perversely she wanted to give him no reason for criticism. Putting everything to the back of her mind, she began to set to work, not letting herself think of anything but the job to hand. She had the memos ready for despatching to all departments when the intercom buzzed.

'Yes, Mr Kruger.' She kept her voice calmly businesslike.

'Would you ask Trevor to come up to my office right away, please, Carolyn?'

'Of course. Shall I send the memos out now?' she asked.

'Finished them already? Good girl. Yes, get them out. No time like the present.'

Carolyn buzzed Trevor and then the office messenger boy. Trevor was the first to arrive, poking his head into her office.

'That was quick.' Carolyn looked up from her memos. 'You must have run up the stairs.'

'Walked quickly.' Trevor grinned as he crossed to her desk. 'Sounded like a royal summons. What's up?'

She grinned. 'Enter the cavalry! Your Southern general is here already.' She indicated the closed door into Mr Kruger's office. 'Half a day early.'

'Wow! He's on the ball.' Trevor sat on the edge of her desk, hitching up one leg of his trousers.

Carolyn scarcely noticed his nearness or the fact that his eyes ran over her. She was a tall girl, just over five seven, and the tailored black suit and pale blue blouse moulded her figure to perfection. She was the most perfectly proportioned woman Trevor knew, long nicely shaped legs, slightly curved hips, fullish bosom. And as far as he could discover she had no social life at all. She never gave any of the guys in the company a shred of encouragement. It was such a waste.

'Who is he?' Trevor asked, and Carolyn studiously kept all expression from her face, her fingers absently straightening the enveloped memos.

'Leith McCabe,' she replied carefully.

'*The* Leith McCabe? Of National Consolidated?' Trevor whistled softly through his teeth. 'Did I say one of the generals? Leith McCabe is the five-star variety!'

'You know him?' Carolyn's eyebrows rose in surprise.

'I know of him. Remember I was with that insurance firm in Melbourne before I came to Kruger's? Well, a friend of mine worked for him then. The family owns companies everywhere. His father, his brother and I think his brother-in-law, they're all involved.' Trevor shook his head. 'He's a financial whiz-kid. Everything he touches turns to gold.'

Carolyn raised her eyebrows again. 'Dare I suggest that bodes well for Kruger's?' she remarked drily.

'Too right it does.' Trevor didn't pick up her note of irony. 'Leith McCabe's just what Kruger's needs. Not that it's old John's fault the company's in dire straits. It's the times. And Peter Kruger hasn't helped. He's an incompetent pain in the neck and not half the man his father is.'

'No,' Carolyn agreed. 'You'd never guess they were even related.'

'Never in a million years. Wonder how Peter's going to take being a humble employee instead of the boss's son?' Trevor shrugged. 'Guess time will tell. And it's not getting me into the lion's den. How's my tie?' He fiddled with the knot.

Carolyn reached across, straightening it for him, and he stood up. For no reason at all she found herself really looking at him, her eyes running over his neat conservative suit, his white shirt and the subdued tonings of his tie. His fairish hair was tidily in place and he wore an unobtrusive-smelling aftershave. Unconsciously she compared him with Leith McCabe, and found Trevor wanting. She supposed they were both just over six feet tall but Trevor wasn't as broad in the shoulders, as——

'Not that bad, am I?' Trevor asked with mock dismay and Carolyn laughed a little self-consciously, a little guiltily.

'You look fine.'

'Thank you, fair lady.' With a flourish he lifted her hand to his lips. 'Wish me luck with the big gun,' he grinned.

A sound behind Trevor had him swinging around as Leith McCabe strode into Carolyn's office. Carolyn met his gaze, looking for some sign that he had overheard Trevor's words. Leith paused, those sharp eyes leaving Carolyn's, taking in Trevor's hasty relinquishment of her hand. A soft flush touched Carolyn's cheeks.

With the two men together she could see that her previous comparison was correct.

She had judged they were of a height and they were, but the similarities ended there. Leith McCabe's whole body exuded hard powerful strength, his body-fitting expensive grey suit moulding his broad shoulders and long muscular legs. The blue of his shirt was reflected in his eyes and beside him Trevor looked pale and lanky. It was hardly Trevor's fault though, Carolyn considered wryly, for Leith Mccabe was a man who would stand out in any crowd.

Trevor recovered his momentary loss of composure and moved forward with his hand out. 'Trevor Green,' he said evenly. 'Carolyn was telling me you'd arrived from Melbourne this morning.'

'Was she?' Leith's voice was evenly controlled as he took Trevor's outstretched hand and slowly turned to look at Carolyn.

She experienced again the sensation of a pair of cool blue eyes impaling her, holding her immobile, imprisoned, and her heartbeat increased. She had the disquieting impression that he was stripping away the shrouds of her soul, laying bare all her very deepest secrets, and once again fear clutched at her, bunching into a tight ball in her stomach so that she had to make a determined effort to prevent her arms from moving to wrap herself in some semblance of protection, to stop him.

Yes, stop him! she screamed silently at herself. But nothing could stop Leith McCabe. He still had that aura of unleashed violence she knew from past experience could errupt with all the force of an exploding volcano. It built up inside him. She'd watched it, almost mesmerised, across that cold and fearsome courtroom.

Stop him! Stop him! Don't allow those blue eyes access to the secret parts you've buried in your farthermost recesses. Carolyn dragged her gaze from his. Walk warily! She had to walk warily, keep out of his way, not draw attention to herself or else he would crush her underfoot as he'd so desperately wanted to do fourteen years ago. And this time she had so much more, so very much more, to lose.

'Go on through,' Leith McCabe said to Trevor. 'I'll be with you in a moment.' He turned back to Carolyn, effectively dismissing the accountant. As Trevor left them Leith stepped closer to Carolyn's desk.

Every nerve in her body tensed until she felt as taut as a bowstring. She was completely rigid. Even her clenched jaw ached. And she could only sit and wait as Leith McCabe held her as effectively captive as a fly stuck on the end of a pin.

'It seems to me, Mrs Allerton, that you would be far better employed to carry out an instruction as soon as it's been given.' His voice was quiet, smoothly controlled and yet so blatantly king of all he surveyed. 'When we asked to see the accountant right away we meant we wanted him in the office immediately, not as soon as you'd finished sitting around gossiping and holding hands with him.'

Carolyn's breath caught in a soundless gasp and a flush of telltale colour washed her face at his insinuation. If he had set out to make her feel like an errant schoolgirl, he had more than succeeded.

'My time in Brisbane at present is extremely limited and therefore valuable as, I'm sure, you'll appreciate,' he finished with a touch of sarcasm. 'It's a pity you don't consider your time here in the office in the same light.'

The unfairness of his accusations churned inside her and she drew a steadying breath. 'Trevor,' she almost bit her tongue, 'Mr Green had only just reached my office and was about to join you when you,' she only just caught herself in time from adding, 'burst in here like some supreme overlord', 'came in here,' she concluded with far more moderation than she was feeling.

Their eyes locked and Carolyn refused to allow him to intimidate her, although he had every advantage. He was standing looking down on her where she sat and there could be no disputing the strength, the overall domination in every inch of his powerful body. But Carolyn's gaze didn't falter even as the cold blue of his eyes deepened stormily. How long they remained motionless, silently warring, she couldn't have hazarded a guess, but Leith McCabe was the first to speak.

'Could you bring in the file on the Nadi project,' he said coldly, his eyes not leaving her face. 'And the Airlie Beach one as well.' He turned on his heel. 'Right away,' he added over his shoulder as he strode across to the connecting door without waiting for Carolyn to acknowledge his direction.

She remained seated gazing at the place where he had been and a tight ball of anger grew unchecked inside her. Good grief! The man was a dictator down to his last toenail! He was a——She pulled herself up short. But she couldn't afford to let him see her chagrin. She shivered, reminding herself not to draw his attention to herself. Any more than she had already, that was!

That same dark head appeared in the doorway as Carolyn was about to stand up. 'Now, Mrs Allerton!' The connecting door closed.

Carolyn pushed her chair back with restrained force and marched across to the filing cabinet, her lips pressed tightly together. Allowing for the harm he could do to herself and Bodie she still doubted whether she would be able to work with him at all should the need arise. Demanding, arrogant——!

She stood with the files in her hands searching for adjectives to describe Leith McCabe when the outer office door opened and their freckled-faced office boy raced in. She gave him the memos to be distributed and, making a forcibly conscious effort to maintain her composure, she tapped on the door and walked into the main office.

Mr Kruger was sitting in his chair, a slight frown furrowing his brow, while Trevor sat stiffly in front of the desk, and he did not look comfortable. Carolyn's eyes went to Leith McCabe. He stood with his hands clasped casually behind his back, to all outward purposes gazing over the panorama of the city, the high-risers, the river, the ribbons of the expressways, the parks.

'Ah, Carolyn.' Mr Kruger smiled at her.

'I've sent young Tom off with the memos,' she said as she crossed to the desk. 'Mr McCabe also wanted these files,' she added evenly, her eyes shifting automatically back to Leith.

'Good,' beamed Mr Kruger as the other man turned and slowly crossed behind the desk to reach out for the thick folders Carolyn was holding.

'Thank you.' Leith McCabe's hand, that same long tanned hand that had covered hers as she sipped the reviving brandy not so long ago, came out towards her and she passed the folders to him.

In her haste to be rid of them, to put space between herself and Leith again, she released the documents before he had taken them and the folders fell on to the desk strewing their contents on to the thick carpet. Carolyn fumbled unsuccessfully to regather them, as did Leith McCabe, and their shoulders touched sending a shock of awareness through Carolyn. Her mouth went dry and a wild surge of heat suffused her body.

Sinking to her knees to hide the colour in her cheeks, she reached for the scattered sheets. But his hand was there before hers, quite accidentally brushing her fingers and her eyes flew of their own accord to meet his. Her senses leapt in response to his nearness and she was filled with a horror that tempered the heat, that left her coldly numb.

Did he feel it, too? Was he aware of the heightened tension, the instaneous gallop of heartbeats, the——

Carolyn dragged her eyes away, but not before she'd seen that split second of reciprocal fire blaze in his. He was quick to disguise it, but she knew it had been there. And what was even more dreadfully mortifying was the fact that he knew she had seen that the brief lapse on his part and the expression on his face, the twist of his lips, had been all self-derisive.

He did not like her no matter that perhaps he found her attractive. Carolyn was, in that moment, so very sure of it, and she was perversely regretful. While she told herself that was the only way it could be, the safest way by far, some small uncontrollable part deep inside her wished——

Wished what? she demanded angrily of herself. That she could allow a man to find her attractive? Want to take her out? Be with her? Kiss her? Make love——? Carolyn swallowed painfully. No, never! All that was part of the past. She'd conditioned herself to exist without the need for anything physical, a man's touch, a caress. Except for Bodie. But Bodie was different. A lump rose in her throat. Oh, Bodie, what can I do?

'Here, Carolyn.' Trevor handed her one of the sheets as she stood up, his kind eyes sympathetic.

Trevor was attracted to her, she knew that. She'd known from the first, but it had been no hardship for her to ignore his tentative advances totally. It would be the same with Leith McCabe. It had to be. And he was after all just a man.

Her knees felt decidedly shaky and she was more than a little breathless as she turned and handed him the papers she had retrieved. She heard herself stammering an apology—and then wished she hadn't, for there in his eyes was that same infuriating hint of mockery.

Without a word he took the files, strode around the desk and sat down between Mr Kruger and Trevor, his whole attention on the typewritten sheets, so obviously dismissing her.

'As I surmised, the Nadi project will have to take precedence.' He flicked through the pages in front of him. 'It will mean a trip out there so that I can evaluate the progress first hand. I find you can only read so much into reports and nine times out of ten they aren't indicative of the true situation. I'll have to schedule a flight to Fiji as soon as I can fit it in.' He frowned thoughtfully at the figures, rubbing one long finger slowly along the side of his jaw.

Carolyn watched him fascinated, the movement of his finger almost mesmerising her. Yes, he had changed, she reflected now that she could observe him rationally—well, a little more rationally. Previously her observations had been based on the physical changes. Now she really looked at him, past his broad shoulders, the way his body had filled out, matured. At twenty-two his boyish good looks had made him every young debutante's dream. But now——

Carolyn swallowed. His face had set in lines of severity, craggy, inflexible. He must be thirty-six, still young, yet already there were streaks of grey in his dark hair. To hold the position he did in NatCon would have taken its toll of him. And he would have to be extremely competent, for according to Trevor NatCon was only the tip of the McCabe family business iceberg. The years of undeviating leadership showed, for his features gave the impression of a man who rarely smiled, whose one direction in life was the daily manipulation of thousands of people, millions of dollars.

But he had smiled at her, when she had almost fainted, Carolyn reminded herself, and that smile had played havoc with her previously punctiliously schooled senses, had found a chink in her armour she hadn't even known existed and had encouraged a response she hadn't dreamed she could be capable of. She shivered involuntarily.

'I'm afraid my son wasn't the right choice for the Nadi project,' John Kruger was saying. 'I thought he needed the chance to prove himself, but unfortunately the lad hasn't handled it very well.'

Lad? Peter Kruger was all of thirty-five, Carolyn thought, and for his father's sake it was time he grew up. Carolyn had never been able to like him, and when she'd refused his repeated offers to take her out he had always sulked or stormed angrily away from her.

John Kruger coughed a little embarrassedly. 'I feel I should say now, Leith, that I'm not asking for any special consideration for my son. I leave the matter entirely up to you, and you have my assurances you'll get no interference from me.'

Carolyn's sympathy went out to her boss and her eyes were still misty with compassion as she turned back to Leith McCabe. The cynical twist of his lips wiped that emotion from her, replacing it with a cold anger. Had the man no humanity? Obviously not.

She dropped her eyes from his. What did you expect? she asked herself derisively. That a merciless twenty-two-year-old would mellow into a charitable thirty-six-year-old?

'I'd better have a copy of these files to take back to Melbourne with me so that I can study them in detail. Perhaps I could have them photocopied?' He didn't look up.

'Carolyn will fix that up for you,' Mr Kruger assured him affably.

'This afternoon, if possible,' added Leith, his dry tone prickling Carolyn.

'Yes, Mr McCabe,' she replied meekly, but he must have caught the undertone in her own voice, for his head lifted fractionally and his eyes narrowed, regarding her sharply. Carolyn schooled her features, her eyelashes falling to disguise any telltale shreds of emotion, before she excused herself and returned to her own office.

Sinking down on to her chair, she bit back a mixture of

anger and despair, directed at Leith McCabe, and at herself. Relax, she admonished herself, and made herself sit back, breathing deeply, steadyingly. Getting herself all het up wasn't going to help at all. She'd just have to stay calm—and unobtrusive.

An hour and a half later the door opened and John Kruger led the other men into Carolyn's office.

'We're off now, Carolyn.' He smiled across at her. 'Leith and I have a luncheon appointment at my club. We should be back in a couple of hours.'

Leith McCabe had his suit jacket slung over his shoulder and he glanced down at his watch, a conservatively styled gold one, quietly expensive, encircling his strong tanned wrist. Carolyn's eyes followed his movements, watched him flick back the cuff of his blue shirt, noted in detail the shape of his hands, the fine dark hair on his wrist, and she blinked, unnerved, as he shrugged into his jacket, the well cut material hugging his broad shoulders.

He turned to Trevor who was hovering in the background. 'Could you be ready at two? We'll collect the engineer and head out to look over the jobs under way in and around the city.'

'Right,' Trevor hurriedly agreed, rubbing his hands together nervously.

'I'm meeting my wife after lunch, Carolyn, so perhaps you could just take any messages,' Mr Kruger directed before following Leith to the door.

'Phew!' Trevor drew his hand theatrically across his brow when they were alone. 'The man's a bloody computerised robot! McCabe, I mean,' he clarified with a grin. 'I've never seen anybody work at that pace.'

'Oh,' Carolyn murmured noncommittally.

'I remember my friend in Melbourne saying Leith McCabe was a human dynamo, now I know what he meant.' Trevor ran a finger agitatedly around the inside of his collar and gave a soft groan. 'And I have to spend the afternoon in his exalted company touring the local sites. Something tells me I'm going to end up totally exhausted trying to keep up with him, let alone getting one step ahead of him.'

'Just try to relax, Trevor,' Carolyn advised him soothingly. 'Let Leith McCabe do the talking. I rather fancy he'd be right in his element being king-pin.'

'He is the king-pin,' Trevor reminded her, his eyes narrowing. 'Handsome devil, the type who has women falling at his feet wherever he goes, wouldn't you say?'

Falling at his feet. Oh, Trevor, if you only knew! What would you say if I told you I'd done just that quite literally only hours ago? Carolyn's lips twisted self-derogatorily for brief seconds before her usual cool mask dropped.

'We can be thankful for a small mercy,' Trevor deftly changed the subject, sensing her withdrawal. 'Leith McCabe is far too big a wheel in NatCon to be able to afford much time for Kruger's. After this initial inspection you can be sure some lesser cog in the machine will be despatched to take us in hand, implementing to the letter all of McCabe's recommendations, of course.'

'I suppose so,' Carolyn frowned thoughtfully, finding it extremely difficult to hide her relief. Trevor was right, Leith McCabe would have too many irons in the fire to be able to babysit a small, by NatCon's standard, construction company that had just been swallowed up into the huge conglomerate.

'Did he say how long he'd be here?' she asked.

'No, not in so many words, but I got the impression it would only be days. I hope so anyway,' Trevor remarked with feeling. 'I know I said we needed NatCon, but Leith McCabe we can do without. He makes me feel like a wayward schoolboy! Let's hope the next few days flash past, preferably painlessly.'

'I'll second that.' Carolyn pulled a sheaf of paper towards her, slipping another sheet into her typewriter. 'So all we can do,' she said lightly to Trevor, 'is keep a low profile until he leaves.'

'Mmm, suppose so.' He watched Carolyn's bent head

as she set her tabs. 'You're not going to start on anything now, are you? It's lunchtime. Why don't we go down to the canteen and drown our sorrows in their poisonous coffee?'

'No, thanks, Trevor.' Carolyn smiled. 'I'll have my lunch here while I'm working. I don't want to be caught with my work unfinished when your big general returns. He might have me court-martialled.'

'He might at that,' Trevor agreed. 'Well, I'll leave you to it. I'm going to prepare myself for this afternoon by having a hearty meal. It may be my last!' he laughed as he closed the door behind him.

Carolyn's composed façade collapsed, her body sagging as she put her head in her hands. Court-martialled. She couldn't have chosen a more apt analogy. If Leith McCabe had had his way fourteen years ago she would have been tossed into jail and the key would have been effectively lost.

And yet she had been innocent. She *had* been innocent. Hadn't she? A wave of the long-remembered, so-familiar guilt crashed over her, tossing her emotions about like a weightless piece of useless flotsam. Nausea rose inside her, almost choking her. But she forced everything to the back of her mind as she had taught herself to do, and the feeling passed. It was the only thing she could do in the battle for self-preservation.

Tiredly, she crossed to the coffee-maker and poured herself a cup, carrying it back to her desk. Almost in a daze she ate her sandwich, scarcely aware it tasted like sawdust. She usually had her lunch in the fresh air of a nearby park, but that was impossible today. She had hours of work ahead of her. At least when she began to type she could lose herself in her work. There would be time later to think about everything, to decide what to do for the best.

Just after four o'clock she took the photocopied files in to Mr Kruger's office.

'Thanks, Carolyn, Leith should be back soon.' Mr

Kruger sat back and put down his pen. 'Quite a day for Kruger's,' he remarked, and sighed tiredly. 'I never dreamed I'd see the day the company went out of the family, but I have to admit this amalgamation has taken a great weight off my shoulders. Things haven't been getting any better.'

'It's the times, Mr Kruger,' Carolyn sympathised. 'Every business is feeling the pinch.'

'It was more than that, Carolyn. We were heading towards bankruptcy.' He shook his head. 'All those men out of work! Some of them have been with me for over thirty years. I couldn't let that happen.' He seemed to draw himself together. 'Besides, my retirement was well overdue. I deserve a rest, don't you think?'

'We'll all miss you,' she told him honestly.

'Thank you, my dear.' He smiled ruefully. 'I have a feeling I'm going to miss all this, too. But NatCon will be the making of Kruger's and Leith's a man after my own heart. He cares about people as well. That's why I couldn't believe my luck when we discussed the takeover and he agreed to my proviso that there would be no jobs lost. Fortune certainly shone on us in the form of NatCon.'

'NatCon won't be losing, Mr Kruger,' Carolyn ventured. 'It will be inheriting your esteem in the industry, the goodwill that goes with Kruger's. Leith McCabe would be very aware of that.'

The old man nodded. 'But goodwill, unfortunately, doesn't pay outstanding accounts,' he reminded her drily. 'Leith's a good man and something of a financial genius. I couldn't even hazard a guess at the size of the group of companies into which Leith has expanded his father's firm. NatCon's only part of it. Of course, it's a family concern, but make no mistake about it, Carolyn, Leith's the boss. He's quite a young man to hold such a responsible position.'

'I suppose so,' she agreed reluctantly, but before she could make any further comment there was a knock on the door and Leith himself strode into the room.

'Leith—how did it go?' John Kruger looked up eagerly.

'Fine, John. Everything was in order so we kept to schedule.'

'Good, good. Would you like a cup of coffee?' the older man asked.

'Please.' Leith sat down in the chair Trevor had used that morning, but unlike the accountant his tall body was relaxed, one long leg crossed over the other.

'Could you see to that, Carolyn?' John Kruger requested, and she nodded, a tiny shiver quivering along the length of her spine as she walked away with the almost tangible touch of a pair of cold blue eyes sliding over her again.

When she returned with the coffee Leith was flicking through the photocopied files. 'Well done,' he said at last. 'Very efficient.'

Her gaze was compelled to meet his and he made no effort to disguise the mockery in their blue depths. Seething inwardly, Carolyn fought down a strong desire to up-end his coffee into his lap. Arrogant, conceited, overbearing——!

'Carolyn's work is always well done,' championed her boss. 'I told you she was the best secretary I've ever had.'

Back at her desk Carolyn angrily spun some company letterhead paper into her typewriter. Because of Mr High-and-Mighty McCabe she was behind with her own work. She glanced at her watch and her lips tightened. With a sigh she began typing swiftly, her fingers flying over the keys. Damn Leith McCabe!

She was so engrossed in her work that Mr Kruger and Leith McCabe were standing beside her desk before she was aware they'd entered her office. John Kruger was shrugging on his light coat.

'Well, we're off,' said her boss as she looked up, her fingers faltering on the typewriter keys. 'We'll see you in the morning. Goodnight, Carolyn.'

'Oh, yes. Goodnight, Mr Kruger.' Her eyes skimmed the knot of Leith McCabe's tie. 'Goodnight,' she said coolly.

'Until tomorrow morning, Mrs Allerton,' said that deep, fluid voice. 'Bright and early,' Leith added as he followed the older man through the outer door.

The traffic was especially heavy as Carolyn drove her ancient blue Gemini along the Old Cleveland Road, or perhaps it just seemed busy because she was running late. She'd forced herself to stay back to finish the last few letters so that at least she would be that far ahead in the morning.

She braked to a halt with the stream of cars and glanced at the time, tapping her fingers impatiently on the steering-wheel as she waited for the interminable change of the red light. Green. Go. The engine of the Gemini hesitated and Carolyn pleaded with it, sighing with relief as it responded sluggishly, picking up as she changed gear.

The car needed a lot of attention, expensive attention. According to the boys next door it should be completely reconditioned. And it was due for a new set of tyres. Tyres. Oh no. She had completely forgotten to drop off the flat tyre. Well, it was too late now. She would have to make time to do it tomorrow. If she had another flat tyre in the meantime——Don't even think about it, she admonished herself as she turned into the Chandler Sporting Venue, a modern complex of international standard which had been built for Brisbane's hosting of the Commonwealth Games.

A soft smile replaced the slight frown on her face as she caught sight of a tall tracksuited figure lounging under the glow of a fluorescent light, nose buried in a magazine. Tall, broad-shouldered, long-legged, nice-looking—well, Carolyn thought so.

She gave a short toot on the horn and the figure turned in her direction, the light shining on his short-cropped blond hair. A huge grin lit his face as he caught sight of her and he picked up his carryall and ran over to the car.

Carolyn leant across the front seat to open the passenger-side door. 'Sorry I'm late, Bodie. Have you been waiting long, love?'

'No, not long. Anyway, I knew you'd be here as soon as you could and I had my magazine to read.' He grinned goodnaturedly as he tossed his bag over into the rear seat of the car. Still smiling, his grey eyes perhaps a shade darker than Carolyn's crinkling at the corners, he slid into the seat beside her and planted a noisy kiss on her cheek.

'Had a good day, Mum?' he asked as he reached for his seatbelt.

CHAPTER TWO

'OH, don't ask!' groaned Carolyn. 'Suffice to say it was one of those days. How about you? Training go well?'

'Mmm, fine. I'm getting my splits spot on and Coach says he's really pleased with me,' Bodie told her as she turned the car out on to the road, heading homewards. 'Oh, and Brett'll be back swimming tomorrow. Mrs Conlon said this afternoon the doctor reckons he can resume training now, so that's great, isn't it?'

Brett Conlon was Bodie's best friend, another promising swimmer, and the boys had known each other since their first swimming lesson eight years ago when they were five-year-olds. Between them, Brett's parents and Carolyn managed a complicated system of ferrying the boys from home to the pool and back again in the morning before breakfast, from home to school, from school to the pool in the afternoon, and home from the pool in the evening.

'And the doctor says he's been really lucky it was just a sprain as it could have been stacks worse. He could have missed the rest of the year.' Bodie sighed. 'Hope nothing like that happens to me. That worries me a bit.'

'Having to miss training?' Carolyn prompted.

'Yes. You know, having something happen when we've planned everything out, the Commonwealth Games and maybe the Olympics two years later if I'm good enough.'

'There's no point in worrying about it, love,' she assured him. 'We just have to take life as it comes. There'll always be setbacks no matter how carefully we lay our plans.'

'I guess so. And I suppose worrying about it is pretty negative. Coach says we have to be positive. Anyway, you didn't tell me what made your day so bad,' he changed the subject.

'A flat tyre to start with, so it was lucky it wasn't my turn to take you and Brett to school. That made me late for work,' Carolyn sighed. 'And it had to be today of all days.'

'Was Mr Kruger mad at you?' Bodie frowned. 'He shouldn't be. You worked late last night.'

'No, not Mr Kruger.' Carolyn paused slightly and realised her fingers had tightened instinctively on the steering-wheel. 'The new boss.'

'You've got a new boss?' Bodie turned to look at her in surprise. 'How come? What happened to Mr Kruger?'

'He's decided to retire and he's sold Kruger's to another company called National Consolidated. The boss of that company is taking over.' 'Oh.' Bodie took in this piece of news thoughtfully. 'You won't lose your job or anything, will you? I mean, lots of people are being made redundant lately.'

'No, nothing like that, I shouldn't think.' She made her tone light, hoping fervently that what she told her son was true. 'It's just a case of replacing Mr Kruger with Mr McCabe.' Would it were that simple, Carolyn wished vehemently.

'Oh,' Bodie repeated. 'What's he like—the new guy?'

Carolyn shrugged, keeping her eyes on the road. 'All right, I guess.' She made a big job of turning into their driveway and negotiating the car into the bay under the high-set house.

Their house was a beautiful rambling old colonial design with verandahs around the front and on both sides. Wide steps led up to latticed doors framed by an arch of finely detailed timber fretwork. The delicate patterned fretwork was repeated in the brackets on each side of the verandah posts and the high sloping corrugated iron roof was also common to the house's style.

Four years ago Carolyn had inherited the house on the death of her maiden aunt who had given her a home when Carolyn came to Queensland six months before Bodie was born. It had always been far too big for them, and when Aunt Josie died Carolyn decided to use some of her savings and the little money Aunt Josie had left her to have the house converted into two self-contained flats. Carolyn and Bodie lived in one flat and they let out the other one. It had worked well and their present tenants had been in the flat for over two years.

The two young men worked nearby and were both studying part-time, one in accountancy and one in engineering. Carolyn considered herself to be fortunate as they were very nice conservative young men.

She unlocked the door and flicked on the living-room light. Throwing her bag on the coffee-table, she kicked off her shoes and sank into a far from new but very comfortable lounge chair.

'Oh, that feels divine!' she sighed, relaxing back into the soft cushions.

'Is this the right moment to ask what's for dinner?' Bodie grinned at her, and she pulled a face at him.

'Dinner's all ready. I put the crockpot on this morning. Five minutes, okay?'

'Okay.' Bodie chuckled and began emptying his large bag, his school books, lunchbox and flask, his towel and swimsuit. 'You didn't exactly tell me much about your new boss,' he remarked as he sorted everything out.

'Not much to tell,' Carolyn replied offhandedly, her head resting back against the chair, her eyes closed. And she'd hoped he'd forgotten. She opened her eyes to find him looking at her and he raised his eyebrows, dark eyebrows for one so fair-haired.

He had a nice open face, a happy face, for he always seemed to be smiling. Even as a baby Carolyn remembered, he'd usually woken with a grin. At thirteen he was tall for his age, as tall as Carolyn, and his swimming training had developed his muscles, his shoulders, his long legs. His blond hair, fairer than Carolyn's, was cut short for convenience as he spent at least four hours in the pool daily and his squarish jaw and determined chin still showed traces of boyishness but were already hinting at the firm lines of manhood.

As she looked at him Carolyn's heart swelled with pride and love. She could see no resemblance to herself in his features, apart perhaps from his grey eyes and fair colouring, or to his father. Bodie was simply himself.

'Doesn't sound as though you're very struck by him,' he was saying. 'Is he a slave driver?'

'Not a bad description,' she replied wryly, and he laughed.

'How old is he? As old as Mr Kruger?'

'No.' Carolyn hesitated. 'In his thirties, I suppose,' she said carefully.

Bodie's interest sharpened. 'What's he look like? Burt Reynolds? Robert Redford? Gene Wilder, maybe?'

Carolyn laughed and pushed herself to her feet, not meeting Bodie's eyes. 'He had me working so hard I didn't have time to notice.' May you bite your tongue for that huge fib, Carolyn Allerton, she reprimanded herself. 'I'll get dinner.' She walked towards the kitchen.

'Is he married?' Bodie asked from behind her, and her step faltered.

She turned slowly around to face him. 'No, I don't

think so. At least no one's mentioned his wife.' Perhaps he was married, she frowned. The thought gave her no pleasure at all. 'Why do you ask, Bodie?'

'Oh, no reason.' Bodie tossed his empty lunchbox into the air and caught it. The corners of his mouth lifted in a grin and he winked at his mother. 'Do you fancy him?'

Carolyn's mouth came open as she gave a gasp of astonishment. Her blood rushed through her veins as her nerve-endings tensed. She was powerless to prevent warm colour from washing her cheeks.

'Fancy him?' she got out, her mouth dry. 'What on earth made you ask that?'

'Oh, well, nothing really.' He shrugged. 'Stranger things have happened, you know.' His grin widened. 'You're blushing, Mum.'

'Bodie.' Carolyn admonished him, half annoyed, half exasperated.

'Gee, Mum, you're great-looking. Why wouldn't a guy——'

'Bodie. I just met the man today and I didn't exactly make the most momentous impression on him.' She continued into the kitchen and took two plates down from the dresser, setting them out on the benchtop with a restrained clatter.

'No worries, Mum. With your looks it would be a piece of cake. If you fancied him he wouldn't stand a chance.' Bodie came up beside her and slid his arms around her, giving her a bearhug. 'All my mates think you're he spunkiest-looking mother they've ever seen.'

'Oh, Bodie!' Carolyn's voice broke and turning she hugged him back. She ruffled his soft hair with her hand. 'I thought you were starving. Sit down and I'll dish up dinner.'

'I'll set the table.' Bodie picked up their place mats and dug the cutlery out of the drawer while Carolyn ladled portions of beef and vegetable casserole out of the slow-cooker.

She passed Bodie his plate and they sat down opposite

each other at the small table, eating in silence for a few moments.

'Mum.' Bodie looked across at Carolyn, his young face serious. 'I've been meaning to tell you for ages that—well, if you want to,' he paused frowning, 'you know, go out on dates or anything—well, I don't mind at all. I mean, I'm not a baby any more and I don't need a sitter, so if you want to go out with anyone you wouldn't have to worry about me.'

'What makes you think I want to go out with anyone?' Carolyn raised her eyebrows. 'I'm quite content with my life the way it is.'

'I'd just like to see you having a good time,' Bodie told her. 'You would go out if you met someone you liked? You wouldn't not go because of me, would you? I reckon you deserve to be happy, Mum.'

'But I am happy, love.' She set down her knife and fork. 'What on earth gave you the idea I wasn't?'

'Oh, nothing.' He looked down at his plate. 'It's just that I kind of realised lately that you never go out, apart from to work or to watch me swim, and you're not old, not really. I mean, twenty-nine's not old.' 'Thank you, kind sir,' Carolyn smiled. 'And will you still think I'm not very old next month when I turn thirty?'

'Thirty.' Bodie pondered exaggeratedly. 'Now thirty sheds quite a different light on the subject.' He grinned at her. 'But twenty-nine's not old, so there's still time.'

She gave him a playful punch and they finished their meal, cleared away and washed the dishes. Afterwards Bodie went to start his homework while Carolyn walked through to the bathroom to have a shower.

Undressing quickly, she adjusted the temperature of the water jets and as she turned to step into the shower recess she caught sight of her naked body in the bathroom mirror. Thirty. She paused, her eyes critically assessing her figure. Her legs were long and shapely and evenly tanned, she noted as she ran her hand over the smooth contours of her thigh, the curve of her hip, the valley of her waist. She turned a little more. Her breasts were full and quite firm. Not the body of a matronly mother of a teenage son, she assured herself. She supposed she was wearing well for a woman on the verge of being considered over the hill.

When she had had Bodie a few months before her seventeenth birthday she had been so ignorantly horrified at the changes in her slim young body, unable to believe that everything would resume its normal shape. Yet it had. Well, almost, she grimaced wryly. Having Bodie had added a new maturity to her figure.

With the enormity of the responsibility of a new baby she had devoured books on child psychology and nutrition, but now she simply ensured that they ate balanced meals. Bodie's swimming training guaranteed he got plenty of healthy exercise and Carolyn often joined him in his programme. Once a week they tried to get out into the country or down to the beach just to relax.

She climbed under the shower, letting the warm water play over her body, feeling some of the tension and tiredness seep out of her. She really was happy with her lot, as she'd told Bodie. She was far too busy, too contented with her life to miss male companionship, to need romance.

A man, she told herself, was not the be-all and end-all of existence. And as far as sex went—well, she fell into bed each night too tired even to give its significance or lack of significance in her life a thought. She ran her hands slowly over her wet body, feeling a tiny curl of something akin to excitement twist in the pit of her stomach.

Fourteen years had drawn a misty haze over her experiences, in fact she barely remembered any of it, let alone any great earth-shattering moments. All she seemed to recall now were disjointed images of the inexperienced fumblings, of pain the first time, of disappointment afterwards and the disbelief as she thought, 'Is that all there is?' She couldn't honestly say she'd missed a physical relationship. Did that make her undersexed, sexless?

Her fingers lingered on her body. What would it be like to have a man make love to her after all this time? Had Bodie's father ever run his hands lingeringly over her skin, caressed and sought out each responsive erotic place? No, there was never time for that. Their lovemaking had always been rushed, furtive, unfulfilling somehow.

Carolyn's hands cupped her breasts as the warm water cascaded over her and without warning she found herself imagining the feel of Leith McCabe's practised hands moving over her and her body jerked like a puppet at the mercy of its string. Her breathing quickened in horror.

What had made her think about him in that context? Why not Trevor? Or Tom Selleck? Why Leith McCabe, of all men? And why had she reacted the way she had? Setting aside the events of fourteen years ago, on today's acquaintance she had no reason even to like the man, let alone be attracted to him. It was all a fanciful misapprehension and she was behaving like an immature schoolgirl.

Hurriedly Carolyn finished her shower and towelled herself dry with unnecessary vigour. She slipped her cotton nightdress over her head and donned a soft towelling robe. Thrusting her feet into her slippers, she walked back into the living-room, deciding she would read for a while until Bodie had finished his homework.

They rose early on the six mornings a week that Bodie trained. Over the years they had developed a routine which was almost second nature to them now. Carolyn drove Bodie and Brett down to the pool by five o'clock, waiting while they put in two hours in the water. Usually she read, or sewed, and occasionally she helped the coach out if he needed an extra time-keeper or supervisor. Bodie got on very well with his coach, an extrovert, who had the uncanny knack of getting the best and then a little more out of his swimmers.

They were back home by seven-thirty, leaving an hour to have breakfast and dress for school and work. Carolyn then dropped Bodie and Brett at school before heading into the city to start work at nine a.m. Brett's mother collected the boys from school in the afternoon and dropped them at the pool where they trained until Carolyn picked them up on her way home from work. The schedule ran like clockwork but didn't leave much spare time for coping with ailing automobiles or flat tyres.

For once the car behaved itself perfectly and Carolyn was quite pleased with herself as she dropped the boys at school, then her tyre at the garage to be repaired. It was five minutes to nine when she parked the Gemini beneath the office block that housed Kruger's. She would prove to Mr High-and-Mighty McCabe that she could, and usually did, get to work on time.

Upstairs she crossed to her desk and looked longingly at the coffee-maker. To her surprise it was switched on, and she walked over and poured herself a cup. Mr Kruger must have wanted an early cup himself, although he rarely drank coffee before mid-morning.

She took a sip, sighing appreciatively, feeling a little of her tension leave her, and turned to walk back to her desk. The figure by the door moved causing her to start and she almost spilled the hot liquid over herself, somehow managing to evade the splashes that fell on to the carpet.

Today Leith McCabe wore a brown suit and a contrasting cream silk shirt. He looked immaculate from the tips of his genuine leather shoes to the top of his dark head. Carolyn's heartbeats were taking their time getting back to normal after the fright he had given her by suddenly and silently appearing in her office. He was so vitally alive, a powerhouse of latent energy, exuding an almost magnetic attraction that arced across the space separating them.

Carolyn tensed apprehensively, all her defences

gathering to protect herself from his potent attraction. He had soundlessly stalked like a tiger into her office when her back was turned, and——

'Do you make a habit of strolling into work when the mood takes you?' he asked evenly, and she stared at him blankly, her voice caught in her throat. 'Well, Mrs Allerton? You do realise it's after nine? Yesterday it was more like half past, so I suppose this morning is something of an improvement. Convenient car trouble again?'

'I did have to drop my tyre at the garage, but——'

'Mrs Allerton,' he cut her short, 'I am considered to be a fair, reasonably considerate employer, but I demand punctuality in my staff.'

'But——' Carolyn began, only to have his raised hand silence her.

'So in future I'd appreciate it if you'd remember I expect you here at your desk at eight-thirty sharp. As of tomorrow.' His blue eyes narrowed. 'And if it means the curtailment of your late nights then I'm afraid that's the price you're going to have to pay to keep your job. Do I make myself clear?'

Carolyn opened her mouth and closed it again, scarcely believing what she was hearing.

'Well, Mrs Allerton?' he asked, maddeningly self-assertive and sure of himself.

'Yes, Mr McCabe,' she lifted her chin, 'I understand perfectly.'

'Good. I've a number of letters on the dictaphone. Bring them in when you've finished them.' With that he turned and strode back into Mr Kruger's office.

Slowly Carolyn walked over to her desk and sat down, her coffee forgotten. Why hadn't she tried to explain to him that because of Bodie's training Mr Kruger had allowed her to start and finish half an hour later than the normal working times? At least he wouldn't have thought she had been deliberately late.

He hadn't exactly given her the time or the opportunity for explanations, she reflected angrily. He'd simply ridden roughshod over her, dictating his policy like some ancient warlord. The obnoxious, arrogant autocrat! So he might be under the illusion he was fair and considerate, but he certainly had no human kindness in him. He probably saw the entire staffs of his many companies as busy little cogs in his big wheel. Oh, how she'd like to bring him down a peg or two!

But she was hardly in a position to do so, she reminded herself. She had too much to lose and above all there was Bodie to consider. Leith McCabe is the boss now, she told herself, and if you want to keep your job you're going to have to get used to that, it seems, if only until things settle back to near normal. As Trevor said he couldn't remain with Kruger's for long, he had too many other commitments, so she'd just have to make the best of it.

Eight-thirty. Okay, Mr Genghis Khan. If you decree eight-thirty then eight-thirty it shall be!

Carolyn groaned softly. That would give them only a half-hour to dress and have breakfast. It threw everything into chaos. She'd have to see Brett's mother this evening and try to arrange something with her until they saw the back of Leith McCabe. Perhaps she could drop Bodie at the Conlons' and Joy could take the boys to school at the usual time.

One thing was for sure, she wasn't going to give Leith McCabe another chance to take her to task for her tardiness tomorrow morning, she'd be darned if she would. With that she set to typing his letters, her anger driving her ruthlessly through her work in no time at all.

Seated at John Kruger's desk, Leith McCabe looked up from the papers he was working on as Carolyn entered the office.

'The letters are ready for your signature,' she said evenly, setting them down on the desktop within his reach.

'Thank you.' He picked them up, his eyes scanning the

top one while she waited for any further instructions. She had plenty of work to be going on with, but Leith McCabe might have other plans for her.

'I want to go over the staff set-up. Could you get the head of the personnel department to come up here and bring——' The phone rang and he stopped talking, motioning to Carolyn to stay where she was as he lifted the receiver. 'McCabe.'

His face broke into a smile that totally changed him, so much so that Carolyn felt herself blink, startled. He looked years younger and his blue eyes sparkled warmly. No one could deny he was every female's image of male attractiveness, the stuff of the best romantic fantasy.

She tried to tell herself she was immune to his charm, his physical appeal, but her own reactions indicated the exact opposite. Sensations she usually kept rigidly at bay clamoured for release. Firmly she kept herself under control, outwardly at least. Her eyes fell to her hands clasped together in front of her as she tried unsuccessfully not to eavesdrop on his conversation which was obviously a personal one.

'Suzy, how are you? What are you doing in Brisbane?' He laughed softly, a deep vibrant sound. 'Are you trying to tell me you needed a break?' His blue eyes danced and he relaxed back in his chair. 'I suppose Mum told you I was here, did she?'

Carolyn grimaced to herself. Had she been the bitchy type she might have been driven to reflect that a man like Leith McCabe couldn't possibly have had a mother. Men like him just evolved.

But she knew he did. Mrs McCabe was fair and petite, and fourteen years ago her face had worn the pale look of despair.

'I don't think I can make it for lunch, I'm afraid,' he was saying as he glanced at his wristwatch. 'But how about dinner tonight?' His long fingers absently twisted the pen he held. 'No, not until tomorrow night. How about you?

'Great, we can fly down together. So,' he leant forward, 'I'll pick you up this evening at, say, seven-thirty. See you then. 'Bye, sweetie.'

He replaced the receiver and the smile lingered on his face as he turned back to Carolyn. 'Now, where were we? Oh, yes, Personnel—I want to look at staff distribution so could you ask,' he paused momentarily, frowning, 'Ian Jordan in Personnel, isn't it?'

Carolyn nodded.

'Ask him to come up, please.'

She hesitated before turning to go, and Leith McCabe's eyebrows rose.

'Is . . . Will Mr Kruger be in today?' she asked softly.

All trace of humour left him and his eyes bored coldly into hers for silent seconds before he spoke. 'No. John's taking a couple of days off. He'll be back on Monday. Unfortunately I have to be in Hobart next week for some important meetings.'

Carolyn's gaze fell from his. Had she imagined the note of dryness in his voice? Did it mean he was aware she would be relieved to see the back of him? Well, it was a fact, she told herself as she returned to her office to call the personnel department. What did he expect? That she would fall under his spell like every other little slave in his multi-million-dollar financial pyramid? Yet she wasn't the same as every other employee and when Leith McCabe remembered her she couldn't see him keeping her on in any capacity.

Word somehow got out, as it usually did, that Ian Jordan was closeted with the new boss and that changes were afoot. The building fairly hummed with speculation. Although the staff were aware of old Mr Kruger's stipulation that there be no loss of jobs everyone was wondering insecurely if it was all just top-level pipe-dreams.

'Have you heard anything yet, Carolyn?' Maggie, one of the typists, cornered her as she passed through their large office on her way back from collecting some specifications. 'About these proposed wholesale sackings?'

'No, I haven't,' Carolyn replied honestly. 'And I should think it's highly unlikely after Mr Kruger's assurances.'

'But where is the old man?' asked another girl amid unhappy murmurings from the rest of the typists. 'Someone said he isn't even here today.'

'No, he isn't,' Carolyn told them hesitantly. 'But he'll be back on Monday.'

'That gives the new broom plenty of time to sweep the place clean,' grimaced the first girl.

'He can sweep me off my feet any time he likes!' Kelly Dean, one of the older typists sauntered forward. She was well known as a collector of male scalps and from all accounts she was a huge success at it.

'He's gorgeous,' continued Kelly, sitting on the edge of a desk, gracefully swinging a nylon-clad leg. 'And unmarried, according to the social column in the southern papers. Lucky you working with him all day, Carolyn. Don't you agree he's the best-looking guy we've had around here in ages?'

Carolyn shifted uncomfortably as half a dozen pairs of eyes watched for her reaction. 'I suppose he is quite nice-looking,' she reluctantly agreed.

Kelly laughed shortly. 'Quite nice-looking!' she mocked. 'Where have you been all your life, Carolyn? I just can't believe it. But then again, maybe you're content to have Trevor Green following you around like a pet spaniel.'

'Oh, shut up, Kelly,' Maggie broke in. 'I can't see that it's any of your business.'

'Well, it's true,' pouted Kelly. 'Trevor Green's had it bad for Carolyn for years and she's still holding him at bay, patting him on the head occasionally to keep him interested. Don't hold out too long, though, Carolyn, you're not getting any younger. Or do you only keep him at arm's length here at work for appearances' sake?'

Carolyn went to move past the other girl, trying not to let Kelly's words goad her into replying to her insinuations. Inwardly she was considerably taken aback at the turn of the conversation. She had been completely unaware that the other girls had been interested enough in her to discuss her, let alone that they had noticed Trevor's attention.

'But I guess now you'll be glad you didn't settle for Trevor Green,' Kelly continued waspishly. 'It leaves you clear for a go at the main chance.'

Carolyn froze, her heartbeats pounding inside her chest. 'What exactly do you mean by that?' she asked quietly.

'Oh, come on, Carolyn!' scoffed Kelly. 'Don't play the innocent. Even you must realise what a fantastic fish the new boss would be if a girl could only land him. I mean, what's a lowly accountant compared to Leith McCabe?'

'Kelly, for heaven's sake! You're a prize bitch,' broke in Maggie.

'What's bitchy about speaking the truth? I'm just voicing what you're all thinking,' said Kelly airily. 'Leith McCabe is a good catch—rich, handsome, downright sexy. What more could a girl want?'

'It may surprise you to know that some of us aren't in the market for a meal-ticket,' Maggie remarked drily.

'Rubbish. Don't kid yourself, Maggie. Anyway, you'd have to go a long way before you'd find a more attractive, sexier meal-ticket than Leith McCabe. Don't you think so, Carolyn?' Kelly continued to probe, her eyes maliciously nettling Carolyn.

'If you're trying to get me to agree the new boss is every woman's dream then I'll go along with that. Superficially,' Carolyn added levelly. 'But looks are only part of it. Depth of character, kindness, mutual respect and some common interests are far more lasting. I'm afraid I'm not very interested in the proverbial pretty face.'

'No. And I suppose with one marriage behind you you wouldn't want to make a mistake with the second,' Kelly said mockingly, and there were one or two gasps from the other girls.

Carolyn lifted her chin. 'No, Kelly, I wouldn't,' she said evenly, her face colouring. 'Now, I'm a little too busy to gossip about the new boss and his so-obvious charms, so if you'll excuse me I have some work to do.'

She went to continue on her way—only to stop dead as a deep voice addressed her from the doorway.

CHAPTER THREE

'AH there you are, Mrs Allerton,' Leith McCabe's tall broad body seemed to dwarf the office and the typists turned as one, eyes round. He strode forward, holding out his hand. 'Are those the specs I was wanting?'

'Yes.' Carolyn relinquished them from nerveless fingers. How long had he been standing at the door? Had he heard their conversation? Her derision? She groaned inwardly.

As usual she could glean nothing from his expression.

'Good.' His blue eyes scanned the identification symbols on the front of the folder before he looked up, taking in the seemingly transfixed group of girls. Even Kelly Dean appeared momentarily at a loss for words.

Then he smiled and Carolyn could feel the change in the atmosphere in the room. She slanted a glance at the other girls, seeing the same wonder repeated in their faces as his charm reached out to them. And who could blame them? Carolyn reflected self-derisively. Didn't he have the same effect on her? Weren't her own eyes drawn inescapably back to his face, drinking in his undeniable attractiveness? He spoke to the girls and they beamed as one, glowing in their collective elation.

His eyes came back to Carolyn, and although the smile still lit his face, his lashes fell, effectively shutting her out. 'Shall we go, Mrs Allerton?' He motioned for Carolyn to precede him and she led the way out into the corridor and along to the lift.

Without a word he reached from behind her to press the button and the material of his suit jacket slid along her bare arm, the sound vibrating loudly in Carolyn's ears, and she stepped jerkily away from him, not meeting his eyes, knowing he would have noticed her sudden movement. However, his words had her eyes darting up at him in horror, her throat constricting painfully.

'I suppose that was a prime example of the "eavesdropper never hearing good of himself" bit,' he remarked drily. 'And should I compliment you on not stooping to gossiping?'

Carolyn couldn't seem to get enough air into her lungs to form a reply. She'd never felt so embarrassed in her life.

'Or for not being foolish enough to be taken in by the proverbial pretty face?' He grimaced. 'Pretty face! Don't you think that was hitting just a little below the belt?'

A dinging sound heralded the arrival of the lift and he motioned her to enter. Carolyn's legs shook and she longed to clutch at the chrome railing for support, but she made no move to do so.

The confining space of the elevator cubicle seemed to draw them together, magnifying the tension that stretched between them like a primed bomb all set to explode. Could he feel it too? Or was it just her own supersensitized body, unaccustomed to the nearness of so very magnetically virile a man?

She swallowed and found her eyes sliding of their own accord from the intricate pattern of the carpet, across to the leather shoes, up the length of his tailored trousers, pausing mesmerised as he shoved his hand into his pocket, drawing the brown material tautly over the contours of his muscular thighs. Carolyn burned, sure she could feel a light film of perspiration break out on her brow.

With his hand in his pocket his unbuttoned jacket fell open showing the cream silk shirt that moulded the flatness of his stomach, the rise of his broad chest. Her eyes climbed higher, drawn by an urgency she was powerless to resist. Up over the tanned column of his throat to the jut of his square jaw, the shadow of the cleft in his chin, his lips, the bottom one slightly fuller, filling Carolyn with a vertiginous yearning to experience the feel of his mouth moving on hers, kissing, caressing, setting her aflame.

Her eyes shot up and locked with his. He had been watching her, probably fully aware of her scrutiny, she realised, and cringed, humiliated, her tongue tip nervously moistening her suddenly dry lips. His gaze fell to her mouth and the tension between them intensified, filling the confined space with its volatility.

She had to say something, anything to relieve some of this repressing tension. 'I'm sorry, Mr McCabe,' she got out, wanting to sink into the floor. Or into his arms. She swallowed guiltily. 'I . . .'

'Are you sorry, Mrs Allerton?' His deep voice seemed to flow into her, race with her own heightened senses to every part of her body. 'Should I prove I'm not just a pretty face, hmm?'

Carolyn couldn't breathe, and she suddenly knew he was going to reach for her, run his hands over her body, assuage the aching need for his touch that blazed inside her.

His hand came out of his pocket and he had actually taken one step towards her when the elevator jerked gently and the doors slid silently open, baring them cruelly, brutally to the outside world.

'Afternoon, sir,' greeted the young office-boy a little nervously. 'Hi, Mrs Allerton,' he added as he stepped into the lift with them.

Somewhat dazedly Carolyn noticed the young boy's ears were a little pink and he shifted edgily. He was not at ease sharing the elevator with the boss. Join the club, she thought a little hysterically. How she wished she was any place but here herself, so near to Leith McCabe. So near and yet so far apart from him.

On Friday evening Leith flew down to Melbourne en route to Tasmania. In the company of the unknown Suzy to whom he'd spoken on the phone, Carolyn reflected as she drove home in the stream of traffic. Well, good luck to her. She deserved a medal, whoever she was.

Today their new boss had driven them all at a torturous pace that left Carolyn totally exhausted but somehow vitally alive. No matter what she thought of him as a person, as far as his business professionalism went he had no equal. He pushed himself harder than he had motivated the staff and looked as bright, as alert and as unruffled as he had first thing in the morning. He was hard at work by the time Carolyn arrived at eight-thirty and one of the receptionists said she'd heard he was in his office at seven o'clock.

After the episode in the elevator Carolyn had well and truly kept her distance from him. She had agonised over the turbulent scene all night having to force herself to go to work this morning. The strain of trying to pretend those few moments of unleashed passion had never existed had made the remainder of the previous afternoon seem like an eternity, even though Leith McCabe had parted from her at their office door and she hadn't seen him before she left for home.

However, she needn't have worked herself up over it. On today's form Leith McCabe had completely forgotten the incident had ever occurred. And she was grateful for that. She was, wasn't she? she asked herself testily as she pulled up for another red traffic light.

But what if——? If what? If the lift hadn't stopped when it did? If the young office-boy hadn't joined them? If Leith McCabe had reached out to her, taken her in his arms, caressed her, kissed her?

The car behind Carolyn's tooted impatiently and she

realised she'd missed the light change. She drove on, mentally admonishing herself. Leith had not kissed her. That was reality. The rest was a figment of her imagination, purely fantasy. She was a fool even to think about it, let alone allow it to happen. To almost happen.

Carolyn sighed. She would put it all, including Leith McCabe, out of her mind. The weekend was ahead of her and Bodie and Brett were competing in a swimming meet down at the Gold Coast, so she had more than enough to keep her mind occupied.

Somehow that wasn't as easy as it had been in the past. Usually she'd been able to shut out unwanted problems until she was ready to cope with them. But she found Leith McCabe and the blustery mixture of antipathy and uncontrollable attraction she experienced in his company seemed to have an unbreakable hold on her thoughts.

But the weekend went all too quickly and it was Monday again. At least Mr Kruger would be back at the office, Carolyn assured herself as she drove to work. Leith would be safely at his important meeting in Hobart.

It was almost like old times, as though Mr Kruger were the head of the company and they had never heard of Leith McCabe. Carolyn found herself relaxing again. When Leith McCabe was here she seemed to be tense all the time, expecting him to appear at any moment. But he was in Tasmania and she was safe.

The phone on her desk rang as she returned from lunch the next day and she hurried across to answer it. She had spent some time in the park and it was a gorgeous day. Her enjoyment still lingered in the lilt of her voice.

'Mr Kruger's office. Carolyn Allerton speaking.'

'McCabe here.' His voice was deeper, impossibly more vibrant on the telephone and it sent shards of purely physical awareness reverberating through her, making her feel faint. She sank weakly on to the chair by her desk and tried to pull herself together.

'Oh—Mr McCabe.' Her mouth went dry and she nervously moistened her lips with her tongue tip. 'I'll put you through to Mr Kruger right away.'

'No, I don't want to talk to John at the moment,' he said evenly. 'I wanted to speak to you.'

Carolyn was absolutely speechless. Her hand tightened on the receiver until her knuckles showed white.

'It's about John's retirement,' he continued. 'I believe you were talking to a few of the department heads about giving John a farewell dinner and I hear there's a collection to buy him a gift?'

'Yes, I thought it would be nice,' Carolyn murmured inanely.

'John's well liked.' He paused. 'A couple of people have mentioned the party to me and I think it's a great idea. Have you any suggestions on what we should get for him?'

'Well, no,' she stammered, her brain refusing to function. It was turning over like a wound-down clock. 'I hadn't given it any thought.' In fact, she'd deliberately tried not to think about the implications of Kruger's without her old boss.

'Then perhaps you could before I return tomorrow.'

'Tomorrow!' her voice whispered huskily, her heart flipping over.

'Tomorrow,' he repeated, and she thought she caught a note of dryness in his deep tone. 'John will be finishing up on Friday, so perhaps you could tee it up with a good catering firm for a dinner on Friday evening—smorgasbord would probably be best. We can use the convention-room on the sixth floor. You'll have to get word to the staff and customers around the city. Ian Jordan can give you a hand there. Do you think you can handle it?'

Those words had her straightening in her chair. She had never given him any reason to question her competence. 'Of course,' she replied coolly.

'I didn't doubt it, Mrs Allerton,' came his reply, and she suspected he was smiling.

The thought of his lips lifting in amusement tore away at her composure and her body sagged weakly again.

'You'd better start the ball rolling right away,' he was saying, and Carolyn rallied enough to pull a face at the receiver.

'Yes, Mr McCabe.' She kept her voice even. 'Do you want me to collect the money for the gift?'

'No. Green can do that.' There was a slight pause. 'Could you see him about it? I haven't time to call him myself.'

'All right.'

'I'll leave you to come up with a suggestion for the gift. Don't worry about the expense. I'll match whatever the staff contributes.'

'That's very generous of you,' Carolyn told him, and then wished she'd had the forethought simply to thank him. Even to her own ears she had sounded just slightly patronising. 'I'll . . . I'll start getting everything organised then,' she added hastily.

'Thank you,' he replied with that same cynicism. 'Until tomorrow, Mrs Allerton.'

The receiver buzzed in her ear and Carolyn slowly replaced it on its cradle.

What was left of the week simply flew by. She saw Leith only fleetingly on his return from Hobart and then just as briefly once or twice a day. When they were together now she wondered if he really saw her, for he seemed more than a little preoccupied, an impression she would have said was totally out of character.

He spent most of his time away from the office, inspecting the local projects. Carolyn also learned from John Kruger that he had other business interests in Brisbane besides Kruger's, so it appeared he was dividing his time between those and Kruger's.

At any rate Carolyn was kept busy with the added work of organising the Friday-night dinner. The caterers had been hired, even at such short notice, and Mr Kruger's wife had been let in on the surprise that was being planned for her husband so she would be coming into town to join the party.

Mr Kruger was a keen bowler, so they had bought him a shiny new set of lawn bowls in a fine leather bag and were having a wristwatch, also part of his retirement gift, engraved by a local jeweller. By Friday morning everything was running according to plan until the jeweller rang apologetically to say he had staff shortages and couldn't possibly deliver the watch as promised. Carolyn groaned. She'd just have to collect the watch herself.

It was just one o'clock by the time she returned, the watch safely in her bag, and she hurried into her office she almost collided with Leith McCabe. Her body touched his, soft curves against hard sinews.

His hands came out to steady her and for one wild tumultuous moment she simply stood transfixed, her breasts nudging his chest, his fingers warm and firm on her bare arms. She became aware of the light spicy tang of his aftershave lotion, the totally masculine fragrance of him that teased her nostrils, making her want to put her mouth to the tanned column of his throat, run her lips along the line of his jaw, find his mouth with her own.

Dear God. What was she thinking of? How could she be such a fool? This was Leith McCabe—remember that. Carolyn stumbled backwards, parting them, and his hands fell, setting her free.

'I'm sorry,' she apologised softly, 'I didn't see you there.'

He inclined his head coolly, his face devoid of expression. The heightened tension that gripped her had to be a one-sided reaction, for he made no sign that her nearness disturbed him in any way.

'I've just collected Mr Kruger's watch so that's all in order now,' Carolyn babbled.

'I thought the jewellers were delivering the watch?' He frowned slightly.

'There was some problem with their staff, so I picked it

up myself, just to be on the safe side.'

'Have you had lunch?' he asked evenly, and she nodded.

'I had a sandwich on the way to the jewellers.'

His eyes held hers momentarily and then he nodded and walked into the hall, away from her.

The party had started by the time Carolyn went down to the sixth floor. She knew Leith and Mr Kruger were still in the office upstairs so she could relax for a while longer.

She had changed out of her plain grey skirt and pale pink blouse into one of her few good outfits. The dark blue dress she was wearing tonight was her favourite. Its lines were simple and it showed her figure to perfection, although the neckline wasn't in the least low-cut. The light soft material felt good against her legs as she walked and the only jewellery she wore was a single strand of pearls and matching pearl ear-studs which had belonged to her aunt.

Mr Kruger was overwhelmed to be honoured by his staff and his response to the speeches was tinged with a little sadness. Carolyn knew he was disappointed his son wasn't there to share his evening, he'd said as much to her before the speeches began.

In truth she had telephoned Peter Kruger when they first started organising the party so that he would have adequate time to fly home from Fiji, but he had opted to pass up attending this special night for his father. His excuses had been thin to say the least, and Carolyn had felt like giving him a piece of her mind, knowing just how disappointed his parents would be. Leith had known of Peter's lack of interest, yet he had thoughtfully given substance to Peter's plea that he was far too busy to leave the project at that stage.

Just before supper Trevor joined Carolyn, slipping his arm around her waist. 'Great night, isn't it?' he asked, his eyes full of open admiration, his fingers giving her a little squeeze. The beer he had been drinking had given him courage, it seemed.

Carolyn tried to move away from him, but he held her fast and, short of creating a scene, she was forced to endure his touch. She had no intention of getting involved with Trevor Green, she never had, and she rather felt she would have to tell him so in the very near future. As it was she could see the interested glances of some of their colleagues.

But a tiny shiver of awareness was wandering down her spine, a sensation she knew had nothing to do with Trevor's hand on her waist. Unable to restrain herself, she turned her head slightly, knowing full well that a pair of piercing blue eyes would be upon her. His gaze went from Trevor's encircling arm to rake her, icy cold and unflatteringly. One corner of his mouth twisted cynically before he turned coldly away.

A spurt of anger raced through her. What right had he to judge her? He didn't even know her, or at least the person she'd become. And if he remembered . . . She suppressed a weakening shudder and tried to concentrate on the conversation around her.

Then, above the sound of the music, the babble of voices, Carolyn's hearing sensitised and she imagined she heard his footsteps coming nearer. Her whole body tensed, poised, waited.

'Time for supper.' Hearing his deep voice beside her was no surprise and Trevor hastily dropped his hand from her waist. 'Mr Kruger would like you to join him and his wife,' he added, and she nodded, excusing herself before she followed his retreating back.

If things had been different could she have taken advantage of this almost tangible awareness that flared between them? She sighed, feeling all at once very confused and unsure of herself, and terribly vulnerable. Because from tonight everything changed. From now on she was on her own with Leith.

There would be no kindly Mr Kruger to help temper the day. If Leith decided to allow her to retain her position as his secretary, she reminded herself. She could understand it if he decided to rearrange and reorganise her into another capacity within the company. She hadn't exactly come through with an unblemished copybook.

Oh, she was efficient enough, she knew that, and perhaps he did find her attractive, but he also made it quite plain that as a person she left him cold. And tonight his glances had been even more icy. So he might decide he wanted another secretary. For some reason this thought didn't fill her with the sense of relief it should have. More like disappointment.

It was midnight by the time Carolyn waved goodbye to Trevor and the last group of the staff to leave. Leith's Jaguar was still in its bay, and with a sigh she slid tiredly into her Gemini and turned on the ignition. The engine fired somewhat unevenly and she flicked on the headlights. However, when she selected reverse gear the engine faltered and died. Oh, no. She frowned at the dashboard and flicked off the lights to try the starter again. Come on, please, she begged the car, to no avail. It refused to fire. Switching off the ignition, Carolyn made a very unladylike remark about cars in general, then specifically her Gemini.

What was she going to do now? At least Bodie wouldn't be worried about her. He was staying with the Conlons for the night. She glanced at her watch, holding it to the light. Ten to twelve. She groaned and tried the engine again, with no luck.

Opening the door, she climbed out. There was nothing else to do but go back up to the office and phone for a taxi. Drat the car. She locked the door and hurried over to the lift, wondering why she bothered about security. A prospective thief wouldn't get far with it.

Pushing the button, she rubbed her arms with her hands, trying not to think about being locked in the car park and being forced to spend the night entombed in its void. She smiled weakly at her vivid imagination. Leith

McCabe was still in the building, so the car park wouldn't be locked up just yet.

She pushed the button again and the lift arrived immediately. The doors slid open and Carolyn started forward as the three men in the lift went to move out. She bit back a cry of fright as strong arms went out to steady her and she found herself staring into Leith McCabe's blue eyes once more.

'Oh,' she breathed, fighting to regain her composure, 'I——' Her voice died away as she became aware of the other two men behind him, looking on in amusement. She swallowed convulsively.

'What's the trouble, Mrs Allerton?' Leith McCabe asked, his voice impersonal, and Carolyn stepped involuntarily backwards. The three men moved from the lift and the soft light fell out into the dimly lit car park. The carpeted cubicle offered Carolyn a retreat and she wished she could step into it and be whisked away.

'My car won't start,' she explained, feeling unaccountably foolish. 'I was going up to the office to phone for a taxi.'

The three men as if on cue headed for her car, led by her boss, and after a slight pause she followed them.

'It did go at first, but then the engine died on me,' she explained as Leith held out his hand for the keys.

'Not out of petrol?' he asked as, not without some difficulty, he folded his long frame into the driver's seat.

'I filled up on the way to work this morning,' Carolyn said succinctly, and caught the shadow of a smile touching his mouth. Perversely she hoped the car wouldn't disgrace her by bursting into life with Leith behind the wheel.

He tried the ignition with no more success than Carolyn had had, and then the bonnet was up and three masculine bodies hung over the engine, tossing around the possible causes of the Gemini's trouble. Eventually Leith straightened and brushed his hands on his handkerchief.

'There doesn't seem to be anything we can do to it tonight in this light,' he said evenly. 'You'll have to leave it here until Monday.'

Carolyn sighed resignedly. She'd known the Gemini's demise was coming, but why tonight? Her headache had reappeared and she yearned for the peaceful comfort of her bed.

'I'll drop you home.'

Her head snapped up as Leith's words penetrated.

'Thank you, but there's really no need. I can easily get a taxi. Driving me home would take you half an hour out of the city.'

'No trouble.' He proceeded to lock her car and handed her the keys.

Carolyn's hand shook as she took them from him, but he'd turned to the other two men.

'I'll see you next week,' he said, and the two men bade them goodnight.

In a bewildered silence Carolyn followed Leith over to the luxurious Jaguar. It glistened opulently even in the dim light and when he held open the door, she slid on to its so-comfortable seat, waiting tensely for her boss to open the driver's side door and join her.

You have to be mad to let this happen, Carolyn Allerton, she admonished herself. Totally mad. Now she had a full half-hour to spend in the confines of the car, so very close to him. The opulent upholstery seemed to fold around her and she couldn't hold back the small sigh of pleasure that escaped her. Wouldn't Bodie love a ride in this? Leith moved and she shot him a nervous look.

'Do you know the Old Cleveland Road?' she asked him a little breathily as he followed the other car out of the car park.

'Vaguely,' he frowned. 'You'd better direct me. I'm not as familiar with the outskirts of the city as I could be.'

At least giving directions dispensed with the need to make conversation, and Carolyn's taut body relaxed just a little. But only until they were safely on the right exit.

Then her hands clasped anxiously at her bag. Her mouth was suddenly dry as he shifted slightly in his seat, reminding her that his hard body was so very close to hers. Each tiny nerve-ending in her own body seemed to quiver its awareness of him.

Of all the men in Australia why did it have to be this one who shook her out of her emotional limbo? Why was it Leith McCabe who set her pulses pounding an agitated tattoo? Leith McCabe! Yearning for, craving his touch. Fourteen years ago his hands had touched her, held her in a painfully punishing grip. In the deep unfathomable recesses of her subconscious did her body masochistically remember that fearful, impassioned moment?

No! No! She had wanted desperately to forget. Just to forget.

She was powerless to prevent her mind flashing back to the scene of their meeting all those years ago. Sitting in the quietness of the high-powered car she went cold as she saw herself leaving the courtroom.

Almost in a complete daze she had walked out through the doors and into the hallway. Her mother, pale and tight-lipped, had ordered her to wait outside while she went to bring the car around, as though she couldn't bear to be seen with her daughter. Carolyn had sensed instinctively that her mother wanted to be rid of her. But that wasn't a feeling that was new to her. It had always been that way between them.

Slowly she had followed her mother's disappearing, disapproving back and she was halfway down the passage when strong fingers had gripped her arm, spinning her around so violently that she had swayed dizzily.

'Are you satisfied now, you little bitch?' he had said thickly, his lips pulled back, his eyes, cold blue eyes, cutting in their anger and detestation. 'No matter what was said in there you'll have to live with the knowledge all your life, won't you?'

Carolyn had shaken her head, her heart pounding in

fear. He was crazy. She had been able to believe in that moment he was capable of killing her with his bare hands. All through the inquest, the long horrible hours, she had watched him across the room, his anger building, his eyes impaling her.

'They should have put you away for life. An eye for an eye. You're nothing but a murderess—a murderess, do you hear me?' He had raised his voice, his fingers biting cruelly into the soft flesh of her arms as he had shaken her.

From somewhere an older man had reached them, an older version of this ruthless young man. It was Leith's father, and he had pulled at those punishing fingers and some of the power left them.

'Son, leave it be. It's done. It's over.'

A woman had joined them, the mother, and she was still crying. And a young girl had supported her, a young girl with the same colouring, the look of Chris, so like him she had to be his sister.

All this Carolyn had taken in automatically as she was held in that brutal grip.

'You killed him. You killed them both. You deserve to suffer, not to go free,' Leith McCabe grated between his teeth, and his mother had sobbed in despair.

'Oh, Leith, please! No good will come of this. Nothing will bring Chris back—nothing.'

'Mum's right, Leith.' The young girl had endorsed her mother's plea, her eyes resting on Carolyn with a pitying dislike. 'Let her go. We've all been through enough.'

'Please.' Carolyn's voice had croaked out of her aching throat. 'I swear I——'

But his fingers had tightened again and she had broken off, crying out in pain. Leith's father had pulled at his son's arms, forcing him to release her, and she had sagged back against the wall. Leith's eyes had still burned into her, cold blue steel searing through her like rapier thrusts.

'You'd better go,' Leith's father had said, his voice

quite calm, and with one last agonised look at Leith McCabe she had gone running out of the building, relief filling her as her mother pulled the car into the kerb. She had flung herself into it as though all the demons her imagination could conjure up were pursuing her.

Now she was here, sitting in Leith McCabe's car, close enough to touch him.

CHAPTER FOUR

FROM out of the past she felt again the remembered pain of his fingers and she couldn't stop herself shivering, rubbing her arms unconsciously with her hands.

'Cold?' he asked, the deep sound of his voice startling her out of her unwelcome thoughts. 'I can adjust the air-conditioning if you are.'

'No, I'm fine. It's really quite warm.' She took a steadying breath. Her whole body was held acutely at his nearness, her senses finely tuned to the movement of his hands on the steering-wheel, the sound of his voice, the way he held his head, the clean male smell of him. Every part of her was sharply honed to him and at that moment, had she had the chance to escape from him, she knew she would have been incapable of moving.

'Have you lived out here long?'

She paused fractionally before replying. 'Thirteen years or so,' she answered cautiously. 'I lived with my aunt and when she died I inherited her house.'

'And have you always lived in Brisbane?'

'No.' Carolyn was becoming increasingly uncomfortable and felt a rush of panic. She had to change the subject. She forced herself to be calm. She was looking too deeply for hidden meanings. It was an innocent query, just idle conversation, she assured herself. If he'd remembered her he would have made some sign before this.

'No, I grew up down south, but I love Brisbane. It's home to me now. I like the weather and the people are more easygoing, I suppose the way of life is a little slower, more natural.' Carolyn's voice faltered as she realised she was babbling in her effort to prevent his questions.

Leith was smiling. 'Spoken like a true converted Queenslander! But I know exactly what you mean. I always enjoyed my sojourns in the Sunshine State.'

'Have you visited Queensland often?' she asked.

'Fairly often, and more often in future. I have a couple of business interests here besides Kruger's, and one in Cairns in the north. In the past few years I've been up to Brisbane at least once a month.'

Once a month. He'd been in the city that often. Carolyn realised she could have crossed his path any time in the past few years, had fate decreed.

'My family enjoy a break on the Gold Coast when they can,' he was saying, and he turned slightly, his eyes meeting hers, holding them momentarily before he gave his attention back to the road. 'My parents, my sister and brother-in-law and two nieces spent a month in our unit at Rainbow Bay earlier in the year, and my mother's still talking about the fine weather and the great time they had.'

'You didn't have a holiday at the Coast with your family?' Carolyn asked carefully.

'No. My young brother and I were in the States at the time.'

'Oh.'

He gave a soft laugh. 'What can I read into that "oh", Mrs Allerton?'

'Nothing exactly.' Carolyn shifted in her seat. The lowered tone of his deep voice was doing disturbing things to her. It wiped out the past, made the present almost intoxicating.

'You sounded very much like my mother,' he said, still amused.

'Everyone needs a break, even——' she stopped, and he laughed again.

'Even me?'

She smiled involuntarily. 'Everyone does.' Suddenly she remembered Bodie's big swimming competition in Melbourne. 'Actually, I have a week's holiday coming up soon. Mr Kruger granted me the time off some months ago. Is it still all right for me to have it?' she asked worriedly. She hadn't given her holiday a thought at the company changeover.

'Of course. As you say, everyone needs a break,' he said drily. He glanced at her again and his eyes seemed to gleam in the dim light from the dash-panel. Carolyn's body responded of its own accord and she wished she could put some space between them. In the car they were far too close to each other, he was far too magnetic and she—well, she was so very vulnerable.

'Have you made any momentous plans for your leave?' he asked.

'Yes.' She paused cautiously again. 'I'm going to Melbourne.'

'Alone?'

'No.' She swallowed. 'With friends.' Well, she rationalised, Joy and Bill Conlon would be going to Melbourne with their son and the swimming team, as was Carolyn, so it wasn't exactly a fib. 'How long is it since you had a holiday?' she asked quickly, turning the conversation away from any more questions about her own plans.

Leith shrugged. 'A while. I guess it's easy to forget about the passage of time when you're on your own and you move about from place to place. You have a tendency to let work become a habit,' he added reflectively, 'and it's a difficult habit to break, especially when you have no ties.'

'Why don't you take some time off when you go over to Fiji?' she suggested. 'Fiji's supposed to be an ideal place for a relaxing holiday. I'm sure I could make some arrangements for you before you go over to take a look at Kruger's project at Nadi. If you'd like,' she finished lamely, cringing at her presumptuousness.

'Are you trying to get rid of me, Mrs Allerton?' he asked mockingly, and Carolyn felt her face flush.

'Oh, no, of course not,' she assured him quickly, afraid that unconsciously she had been doing just that. 'I was simply—well, making a suggestion.'

He was smiling. 'And I just might give that suggestion some thought.'

His tone held a note she couldn't quite fathom, and her tension increased. In this more relaxed, more intimate situation away from the office his attraction was having an even more potent effect on her. She turned to glance out of the window of the car, her stomach churning with an indescribable and unexplainable excitement.

'Oh no.' Her eyes took in the passing landmarks and she realised she'd allowed him to drive past her turn-off. 'We should have taken the last right turn, by the little shop. I'm so sorry, I should have been watching.'

Leith slowed the Jaguar and made an effortless U-turn when the light traffic cleared.

'This one here,' Carolyn pointed out as they retraced their steps. 'And then the second street on the left. I can't think how I came to miss it.'

You have to be joking, Carolyn Allerton, she chided herself. When you're near Leith McCabe you don't know if you're on your head or your heels. And this close to him . . .

'Third house on the left,' she said hurriedly as he turned into her street.

The luxurious car came to a halt in front of the rambling old house. Only a faint light glowed in a front window of the other flat.

Carolyn turned to thank Leith McCabe for the lift, but he was out of the car and already striding around to open her door for her. Grateful for the screening darkness, she climbed stiffly out on to the footpath. Her colour had risen again and her blood pounded excitedly through her veins.

'Thank you very much for driving me home,' she began breathily. 'I appreciate it.' Should she ask him if he'd like a cup of coffee? No. That would be far too dangerous.

'My pleasure,' he replied easily.

Carolyn swallowed. 'Goodnight.'

'I'll see you to your door.' He turned and took her elbow, moving her towards the gate before she had realised his intention.

'Oh, no, that's all right,' she assured him hurriedly, drawing back from him. 'I don't want to keep you. It's late and you'll be wanting to get back to the city.'

'A few more minutes won't make much difference.' He had the gate open now and Carolyn could only walk before him up the cement path.

At least his hand had gone from her arm, even if the sensation of the feel of his fingers on her skin remained, and she had to prevent herself from breaking into a run, along the path, up the steps to safety.

In her restrained haste she almost tripped as she caught her heel on the wide step. His hand reached out instinctively to steady her and her fingers clutched at the smooth material in the sleeve of his jacket. Just as quickly she moved away from him, blindly groping for the knob on the lattice door, swinging it open. And there was the door to their half of the house. Sanctuary.

'Thank you, Mr McCabe.' She turned on the top step, effectively blocking his way on to the verandah, and even though he stood on the step below her their eyes were not on a level. He was still taller than she was and she had to look up to meet his shadowed gaze.

At that moment her keys fell from her shaking fingers and clattered on to the step at her feet. She went down to retrieve them as he did and their fingers touched, sending tingling shivers racing up her arm to wash over her whole body, the sensations building up into a tide of wanting she had never before experienced.

She was poised there, on her haunches, unable to move a muscle, her eyes wide, locked with his as they gleamed in the shroud of the balmy night. Time had to be standing still for nothing seemed to move, no blade of grass or leaf or tree. Then Carolyn heard him catch his breath and his fingers folded around hers, tightened until the sharpness of the keys pressed into her hand.

'Carolyn.' He said her name softly, hardly above a whisper, and his voice seemed to catch painfully in his throat. The deep vibrant sound aroused her senses so sharply and violently she thought she would faint.

She felt herself sway forwards, drawn towards him, aching to feel his arms around her. Her lips sought his, compelled to taste their potent possession.

With brutal suddenness the verandah light flicked on, the abrupt brightness bursting over them, drowning them, freezing them like a douche of cold water. The twin door to Carolyn's flat opened and a tousled dark head appeared in the aperture.

'Oh, it's you, Carolyn. Thought we were being burgled.' Greg, from the flat next door, stepped through the doorway clad only in short low-slung pyjama bottoms. His gaze took in the still crouched figures of Carolyn and the man so close to her.

Greg's appearance stung her into action and she stood up on stiff legs, her keys forgotten. Leith McCabe slowly straightened too, his eyes going from Carolyn's flushed face to Greg's pyjama-clad near-nakedness. His eyes still gleamed, but now they were that cold steely blue, icy and uncompromising and his lips thinned cynically.

'Your keys.' He'd picked them up and he held them out to Carolyn, dropping them into her outstretched hand, not touching her.

'Thank you,' she said huskily, her mind turning over his obvious misconceptions with a disbelieving, painful slowness. Surely he didn't imagine that she and Greg . . .?

'Goodnight, Mrs Allerton.' He nodded coldly in Greg's direction and then he was gone, striding down the path to the car.

Carolyn couldn't move. She stood numbly, her fingers wrapped convulsively around her keys as the Jaguar's red tail lights disappeared around the corner. And she wanted desperately to call him back, explain.

'Hey, I didn't interrupt anything, did I, Carolyn?' Greg's voice came concernedly from behind her, and she pulled herself together before she turned around to face him.

'No, of course not.' She managed a light laugh. 'My car gave up the ghost and I got a lift home.'

Greg was watching her and she schooled her features, holding his gaze.

'Bit of a dark and smouldery type. Who was he?'

Carolyn grimaced. 'The new boss, Mr McCabe.'

'Oh yeah?' Greg yawned. 'Bodie told me Kruger's had been sold. All I can say is for your sake I hope he's not as forbidding as he looks. He's not as easygoing as old Mr Kruger, I'll bet.'

'No, not exactly,' Carolyn agreed, and shrugged. 'But he has other interests besides Kruger's, so he isn't always at the office.'

'Ah, the tycoon bit,' Greg nodded understandingly. 'Anyway, what's gone wrong with the car this time?' he asked as Carolyn stepped over to unlock her door.

'About everything I'd say.' She sighed, relieved the subject had been changed. 'But I'm going to put it out of my mind until Monday.'

'Good idea.' He shook his head. 'You know, you might be better cutting your losses and trading it in, it needs heaps of work done on it.'

'Mmm. I guess I'll have to make a decision about it one way or the other.' She grinned crookedly. 'But not until Monday.'

Greg laughed. 'Right. See you, Carolyn. 'Night!'

'Goodnight, Greg.' Carolyn went inside, felt for the light-switch and flicked it on. She was home at last. She leant back against the closed door and her body sagged limply.

Now she was alone that one moment on the step, that totally horrifying, oh, so completely electrifying moment when she and Leith had been held motionless, bound together in a web of awareness, came flooding back with vivid clarity. And the way he'd said her name—not Mrs Allerton, but using her Christian name, his deep vibrant tone dissolving all her inhibitions so easily. Had she imagined it? No, she'd heard him say it. Carolyn. In that low, liquid, so-arousing voice.

She shivered. Her reactions had been explosive, instantaneously explosive.

If only Greg hadn't chosen that precise moment to switch on the verandah light! If he hadn't they would have kissed. His lips would have touched hers, his body would have moulded itself to hers, fused with her body. She had wanted it so very badly——

There can be no future in it, she told herself forcefully. He would never be able to forgive her for what he thought she'd done. Never. And Greg interrupting them was for the best, deep down she knew that. But what would one kiss out of time have mattered? It would have been something to remember . . . If only . . .

Eventually she forced herself to move, to walk towards her bedroom, her limbs as stiff and stilted as a puppet's. And all the while she could only repeat despairingly over and over to herself, 'Why Leith McCabe? Why did it have to be him?'

A tow-truck from the Royal Automobile Club came along on Monday morning and took Carolyn's Gemini to the repair shop, but it was lunchtime before they rang to report on the problem. Or problems, Carolyn reflected ruefully.

She had had to leave her share of delivering the boys to training and school to Joy Conlon again as she had to catch a bus in to work. Their whole schedule was thrown out of the window and would be until Carolyn's car was back on the road and everything returned to normal.

She replaced the telephone receiver on to its cradle and pursed her lips. Had she made the right decision or was she simply postponing the inevitable, throwing good money after bad? She closed her eyes, moving her fingertips soothingly over her temples, trying to ease the tension.

'Headache, Mrs Allerton?'

Her fingers stilled and she sat up stiffly, her face set expressionlessly. His greeting that morning had been brusque before he'd issued his orders and disappeared into his office. From his desk he had been driving everyone at top pace all morning.

'No, I'm fine,' she replied, not meeting his eyes. She could feel him watching her and she waited with outward composure for his next lot of instructions. Inwardly she was a mass of quivering tingles of excitement. God, if he only knew the effect he had on her!

'Have you heard anything about your car?'

Surprised, Carolyn looked up at him, then and gave a nod of her head. 'Yes, they just rang. It needs,' she paused, 'quite a bit of work done on it, but they said I'd have it by Wednesday.' She omitted to tell him the mechanic had recommended a major overhaul which would have taken at least two weeks and cost the earth. She had decided on the alternative, to have it patched up, and later, after Christmas perhaps, she'd get it completely reconditioned.

'I've known for some time that it needed attention. Greg from the flat next door to mine, you met him the other night—well, he told me ages ago the car should be overhauled.'

Leith's expression gave away none of his thoughts, so if she had expected a reaction to her explanation about

Greg's presence she was disappointed. He crossed to her desk and taking a set of car keys from his pocket he placed them beside her typewriter.

'There's a spare in the car pool, a yellow Sigma. You may as well use it until yours is repaired,' he said evenly. 'I've arranged for it to be left in the car park for you this afternoon.'

Carolyn's lips parted in astonishment. 'Oh, but I couldn't.' She swallowed. 'What if something happened to it?'

'Nothing will.' He turned towards the door to his office. 'Could you get Peter Kruger in Nadi?'

'He might be out of the office,' she started to say, but the door had closed on his broad back.

Carolyn picked up the car keys and her fingers folded around them. She couldn't understand him. All morning he had treated her as though she weren't there; he had simply issued orders in her direction. She had seethed at his superciliousness. If his attitude had anything to do with Friday evening then he had no right or reason to pass judgement on her. Perhaps it had seemed as though she and Greg might have been more than the friends they were, but what business was it of his how and with whom she spent her time outside working hours? With his looks and position he wouldn't have been celibate. He didn't have the appearance of a man who went without a woman's company for long. And the mysterious Suzy was obviously on very friendly terms with him.

Carolyn trembled slightly, her imagination conjuring up a picture of Leith's hands caressing her own body, his long firm nakedness merged with hers, and she could almost feel the sensation. And then just as vividly she saw him with another woman, his hands on her, kissing her, and she closed her eyes at the stab of pain that thought generated.

You fool, Carolyn Allerton, she berated herself, you blind misguided fool! How could you allow yourself to fall in love with him? That was the reason for her sleepless tossing and turning, her soul-searching since Friday night. The realisation had been there all the time, but she'd refused to allow herself to acknowledge it. She was in love with her new boss.

No, she couldn't be. It was impossible. She didn't even like him. You had to care for someone to fall in love with him, didn't you?

Carolyn shook her head disturbedly. What did she know of love, the love between a man and a woman? The only love she'd known in her life was the fierce tender maternal bond that existed between herself and Bodie. That love had been born the moment she'd held him in her arms.

Her own childhood had been completely loveless. Her parents had had little time for her. She was the reason her mother had married her father and neither of them had wanted the marriage or the responsibility of a child, as her mother had reminded her regularly. However, in those days if a girl became pregnant she went to the altar as quickly as she could.

Carolyn had grown up in the midst of the fighting and the bickering until her father had left them, divorcing her mother and marrying his secretary. He had been more than relieved to leave Carolyn with her mother.

On their own Carolyn had hoped for an end to the unpleasantness, but for a year after the divorce her mother had turned to bitter cynicism, until she had met Joe Barton, a quiet no-nonsense type of man, and a few months later they had been married. Although Carolyn's mother and her stepfather had seemed to be quite happy in their marriage Joe Barton had not been enthusiastic about a ready-made family, and at thirteen years old, insecure and vulnerable, Carolyn had sensed this. Not that her stepfather had been cruel, rather he'd treated her as though she weren't there.

Her stepbrother and stepsister had been born within two years. Now, nearly twenty years on, she could see her mother must have had her hands full with two babies after so long, but at the time she had felt only the continued rejection. Her mother had had even less inclination to listen.

So Carolyn had spent more and more time with a group of teenagers from her school. The leader of the gang, the tallest, oldest, most popular youth, had noticed her and she had become his girl. At last she belonged. And any qualms, any misgivings she had had over some of their escapades, their behaviour, she had pushed to the back of her mind. It had been so easy to justify everything when you were part of a group, a family almost, for the first time. Her mother's rejection had been a little easier to bear when she had Bodie's father and the rest of the gang.

She had loved Bodie's father then. At the time she would have said she would love him for ever. In retrospect she could see it had been a type of hero-worship. She had been grateful for his attention, that he had chosen her when he could have had any girl he wanted. He was the first person to draw her out of obscurity, make her feel she was someone special. Her heart had swelled with it as she rode on the back of his immaculate, highly polished motor-cycle, her arms wrapped around his thin youthful body.

It would be so different to slide her arms around Leith's solidness, to feel the hardness of male muscles, the warmth of his body. Carolyn groaned softly. What was wrong with her? It had to be biological, purely physical attraction. Maybe any presentable male would have done. Untrue, said a voice inside her. Trevor Green was presentable, and attractive, and she had never felt an even momentary attraction to him.

Then the intercom buzzed and Leith's deep voice was reminding her shortly that he wanted to speak to Fiji today and not next week. Taking a deep breath, Carolyn reached shakily for the phone.

On Tuesday night Leith flew back to Melbourne leaving her with enough work to keep her nose to the grindstone for a week, let alone the two days he planned on being away from the office. At least it left no time for brooding, for she was so tired by the time she got home in the evening she was inclined to doze over her book while Bodie did his homework.

On top of it all the mechanic from the garage rang her on Wednesday morning to tell her most apologetically that they were waiting for a part and couldn't see her car being ready before Monday or Tuesday of the following week. Carolyn groaned. Now what should she do? Leith had been kind enough to lend her the company car until Wednesday and he wasn't here for her to ask his permission to keep the car a few days longer. Besides, the number he had given her to contact him had been only for emergencies.

She rang the car pool attendant to check that the car was still free, and when he assured her it was she reluctantly drove it home again on Wednesday. It was such a pleasure to drive a car that didn't stall at stop-lights or lose power for no reason whenever it chose to be cantankerous.

When she'd arrived home in the car on Monday Bodie had raised his eyebrows in surprise.

'You mean Mr McCabe just gave you the car to use, without you even asking him?' He was incredulous.

Carolyn nodded, not quite meeting his eyes.

'Gee. He can't be all that bad, Mum. I think it's pretty decent of him.'

Decent, yes, she mused, sensible, no. The fact that she was using the car had not gone unnoticed, she was aware of that, so heaven only knew what choice little rumours would be doing the rounds of the building.

Right on five o'clock on Thursday evening Carolyn finished off the letter she was typing. She had been expecting Leith to arrive for the past hour and when the outer office door swung open her body tensed, only to feel a disappointing release when Trevor Green crossed to her desk.

'Hello, Carolyn. I hoped I'd catch you before you left.' He motioned towards the connecting door as she busied herself covering her typewriter and tidying away her work. 'When's the boss due back?'

'This afternoon, but he must have been held up.' Tiredly Carolyn massaged the back of her neck, tensing her stiff spine. 'Mmm, I'm looking forward to getting home and putting my feet up without having to answer a telephone or type another letter!'

'Had one of those days?' Trevor commiserated.

'Sure have.' She walked across and slipped her arms into the light mulberry jacket that matched her skirt and paler mulberry blouse. 'Are you leaving now?' she asked Trevor as she took her shoulder bag from her drawer. She didn't want to hurry him, but she was far too tired to stand around talking to him, and besides, Leith could arrive any moment.

'Not yet, unfortunately. I've got another couple of hours' work to put in today.' He shifted on his feet a little nervously. 'I just wondered if you were free tomorrow evening you might like to come out to dinner with me.'

'Oh, Trevor, thank you for the invitation, but I'm afraid I can't tomorrow night. I already have something on and—well, I can't change it,' she finished lamely. Bodie was swimming, but she didn't tell Trevor that.

Trevor's face turned a little pink. 'I see.' His eyes went automatically to the door leading into Leith's office and his lips thinned. 'Maybe some other time.'

'Yes,' Carolyn replied stiffly. It appeared the rumours were circulating and there was no mistaking the conclusions Trevor had drawn. She swallowed a spurt of anger as she felt herself flushing.

'Someone said you were driving one of the company cars,' Trevor ventured, and she met his gaze unwaveringly.

'My car's in for repair and Lei . . .' She caught his name back, but Trevor hadn't missed her slip of the tongue. Why had she used his first name? She never allowed herself to think of him as Leith. 'Mr McCabe,' she continued hurriedly, 'was kind enough to lend me the car until mine's repaired. Now, I must be off, Trevor. I'll see you tomorrow.'

'Yes.' His eyes held hers for a moment before he smiled ruefully. 'And I guess I'll just have to pick an evening you're free, won't I?'

On Friday morning Carolyn hurried up to her office mentally preparing herself to face Leith. Her nerves seemed to be more finely honed, and this hadn't been helped by the fact that tonight Bodie was swimming in a major meet.

Although usually calmly philosophical about his swimming competitions, Bodie did suffer a little from nerves the morning of a race day. He laughingly said it was like sitting for an examination. He was sure he'd studied and learned all the answers, but there was always that threat of the unexpected.

Carolyn knew he'd been full of nervous excitement by the way he'd prowled about the house before breakfast, double and triple-checking his swimming-bag which he'd packed the night before. However, he had eaten his breakfast of freshly squeezed orange juice and his favourite baked beans on toast with his usual relish.

She was still thinking about him when she entered her office, her eyes going immediately to the closed door. When she reached her desk she could see Leith had been into the office already.

Shedding her jacket, she switched on the dictaphone before crossing to make a cup of coffee. His deep voice sent tiny shivers down her spine, and as she sat down he informed her in his businesslike tone that he would be up at the North Coast construction site all day, and would return to the office that evening. He gave the number where he could be reached at lunchtime. Before she had time to digest this piece of information his next words caused her to freeze with her coffee-cup halfway to her lips.

'So I'll collect you about nine o'clock on Sunday morning. We could be away for the entire week.'

Shakily Carolyn reached over and stopped the machine, rewinding it, playing it again.

He couldn't be serious! She couldn't go to Fiji with him. Not with *him*.

She stood up and paced the carpet, not hearing the letter Leith McCabe's voice was dictating. She was shaking in her agitation.

Why would he possibly need her with him when he went to check over the Nadi project? If he needed notes taken surely Peter Kruger could find him someone capable of doing that. Anyone could do it. It wasn't imperative that she went along. He'd read the Nadi file, and would know more about the project than she would. Besides, a week in Fiji with him would be——

Bodie's championships. She couldn't miss those, especially not Bodie's eight hundred metres freestyle event on Sunday. He was so looking forward to competing in that one, and she never missed his races. It was the prefect excuse. Leith would understand, wouldn't he? And they were to be in Melbourne the following week when she had her leave.

Carolyn sat down again and shut off the machine. There was nothing else for it. She'd have to tell him it was impossible for her to accompany him. She would have to telephone him. Her heart sank and she gently rubbed her temples with her fingertips in an effort to relieve some of her tension.

For the rest of the morning she tried valiantly to concentrate on her work, but she was having an uphill battle. Her fingers faltered on her typewriter keys while part of her couldn't prevent herself from imagining, conjuring up a picture of herself and Leith on a white beach beneath breeze-stirred palm trees on a sunny Pacific island.

The time to put through her call came all too soon and it took some time to locate Leith. All the while her nerves stretched to breaking point and her fingers ached from clutching the receiver so tensely.

'McCabe.' His tone was curt and unapproachable.

'It's Carolyn Allerton here, Mr McCabe,' she began, her throat contracting painfully. 'I'm sorry to disturb you, but I—well,' she swallowed, and then her words came out in a rush, 'I won't be able to come to Fiji. I have—I've made plans for this weekend I can't change.'

There was a moment's silence that stretched until Carolyn wondered if their connection had been broken.

'Plans are made to be changed,' came his dry voice.

'I'm sorry, Mr McCabe. I can't this weekend,' Carolyn repeated thinly.

'Surely your job's worth more to you than a romance, no matter how torrid it is,' he remarked with scathing cynicism.

She gasped. 'It has nothing to do with a romance!' she spluttered indignantly. 'It's . . . I've made a commitment to be . . . There's someone I can't disappoint. It's very important to me.' Her voice broke slightly and she swallowed again. 'And you did say I could take my leave the week after next.'

There was a noise she couldn't identify in the background and then he spoke, not bothering to disguise his impatience.

'We'll talk about this later. I'm due in a meeting five minutes ago. I'll see you before you leave this afternoon.'

With that the line went dead, and Carolyn was left staring impotently at the receiver.

'I'll have a quick shower,' Carolyn called to Bodie as she hurried along the hallway.

'Don't rush, Mum, we've got plenty of time,' Bodie assured her.

Leith had not arrived back at the office before Carolyn left dead on five o'clock. Perhaps he had expected her to wait for him, but with the swimming championships starting at seven Carolyn needed to be home as early as possible. That she had been relieved not to have seen her boss was an understatement. She knew she was suffering from an acute case of cowardice.

She had left him a note on top of his other messages telling him she had been unable to wait for him and that he could telephone her at home before six-fifteen that evening or tomorrow morning and she would explain. Although quite how she was going to do that she hadn't yet decided.

Switching off the shower, she slid the glass partition open and reached for her towel, hastily rubbing herself dry. Shrugging into her towelling bathrobe, she tied the belt around her waist and opened the bathroom door. As she stepped barefooted into the hallway the doorbell pealed.

'I'll get it!' called Bodie, obviously thinking Carolyn was still in the shower, and she heard him open the door.

'Yes, may I help you?' he was asking politely as Carolyn walked towards the front of the house.

'I believe Carolyn Allerton lives here?' The sound of the deep vibrant voice Carolyn recognised immediately had her jerking to a stop, her heartbeats tripping over themselves in a rush of shocked anticipation as she stood poised, transfixed.

'Yes, she does,' Bodie acknowledged, sounding a little puzzled.

'May I see her?' Leith asked evenly.

'Well, I guess so.' Bodie paused uncertainly. 'Who shall I say is calling?' his young voice enquired formally.

'Leith McCabe.'

'Oh.' Bodie's voice was now all smiles. 'You're the new boss. Come on in and I'll tell her you're here. She's probably out of the shower, I should think.'

The sound of footsteps moved into the vestibule and Carolyn was galvanised into action, hurrying forward, forgetting she was dressed only in a clinging, figure-moulding bathrobe.

'Perhaps you'd like to wait in here, Mr McCabe.'

Bodie was motioning Leith McCabe into the living-room as Carolyn rounded the corner of the hallway.

They both turned to face her and she stopped just as suddenly, her hand going out to the wall for support, something tangible she could reach out and touch, to remind her that this was reality, actually happening, and not some crazy fantasy. Leith's blue eyes were shuttered, his eyelashes shielding their expression, while Bodie's face was wreathed in smiles.

'Mr McCabe's here, Mum,' he said unnecessarily, and Carolyn watched Leith's gaze swing straight to her son.

CHAPTER FIVE

'MR MCCABE.' Carolyn made her shaking legs propel her forward until she was standing slightly behind Bodie. Her hands went out to clasp his shoulders, her fingers tightening until Bodie moved a little in protest. She forced her hold on him to relax, although she wanted to push him behind her, shield him with her body.

'What . . . what can I do for you?' she got out.

Leith's eyes flashed to Carolyn and then returned to Bodie, and she could see that Bodie's presence had thrown him. For once the great Leith McCabe's self-possession was shaken.

'My plane was late back, so I missed you at the office,' he said almost absently, and then he seemed to gather himself together. 'I wanted to sort out this business about the Fijian trip.'

'I'm sorry about that. I expected you to phone me.' Carolyn steeled herself. 'I can't possibly go with you.'

Bodie's interested gaze went from one to the other.

'I was unaware you had a family,' Leith remarked, not commenting on what she had said.

'And Mum doesn't look old enough to have a kid my

age,' Bodie grinned. 'Everyone tells her that.'

He glanced sideways at Carolyn, his smile still lighting his face, and she felt a rush of love for him, had to stop herself hugging him to her. A faint smile lifted the corners of her mouth as Bodie turned back to Leith.

'I'm Bodie Allerton, Mr McCabe,' Bodie held out his hand. 'Mum's told me all about you.'

Leith solemnly shook hands with Bodie, but his eyes as they swung to meet Carolyn's held a slightly mocking light. Obviously he had fully regained his composure. Carolyn just wished she had.

'Has she now?' he queried, and Bodie chuckled.

'It's okay. Most of it's been good.'

Leith raised one dark eyebrow before he inclined his head. 'I'm pleased to hear it.' A faint smile shadowed his firm lips, and Carolyn swallowed nervously.

'I'm very sorry, Mr McCabe, but we were just about to go out, so I'm afraid I . . .'

'I won't keep you long.' His eyes left her face, slid downwards over her figure so subtly moulded by the terry-towelling bathrobe, and Carolyn stiffened, fighting the almost overwhelming urge to let her fingers draw together the plunging V of the lapels. She didn't want him to know the tremendous effect those piercing blue eyes had on her.

'About the trip to Fiji,' Leith was saying, 'I prefer to have you with me as you're familiar with the whole project. I haven't the time to fill in anyone else, if someone suitable is available in Nadi.'

Bodie was frowning and Carolyn broke in, 'I'm afraid it's too short notice.'

'I didn't know until Thursday evening that I'd be able to spare the time to go out there next week.' He held Carolyn's gaze and she could feel the will of iron he exuded. 'I may not get an opportunity again for some time so it has to be next week.'

She could now feel herself weakening. But she mustn't. She couldn't go with him. 'You could take one of the girls from the typing pool. I'm sure Kelly Dean——'

'Carolyn, I want you on this job.' So caught up with each other, with the silent unspoken battle were they, neither of them noticed he had used her Christian name. A look of irritation crossed his face. 'What could be so important that you can't postpone it for a week?'

'Mum, I can stay at Brett's if you're worried about me,' Bodie put in.

'It's all right, love.' Carolyn squeezed his shoulder warningly. 'Perhaps you could go and make Mr McCabe a cup of coffee.

Okay. But——'

'Go on, Bodie.' Carolyn gave him a gentle push and he went reluctantly through to the kitchen to do as she asked him.

'Would you care to come into the living-room?' She motioned to the doorway off to her right, colouring a little when she realised she had kept her boss standing in the small vestibule.

He stood back politely for her to lead the way and she walked stiffly into the room, making sure she kept as much space as possible between them. She watched his eyes skim the furniture, the large comfortable chairs, Bodie's desk with his school books piled on top of it, and the corner of the room where most of Bodie's trophies, medals and certificates were on display.

'About Sunday,' Carolyn began, only to be interrupted by the telephone's strident ring. It was out in the hallway, and she excused herself, walking exasperatedly out to pick up the receiver.

'Hello.' Her voice was a trifle sharp and she wished fervently that the whole world would go away and leave her alone.

'Carolyn? It's Trevor. I thought I might have missed you.'

'No, but I'm leaving quite soon.' Carolyn fought down an irritated urge to simply hang up the phone but of course she couldn't do that.

'Okay, I won't hold you up. I just wondered if you knew where I could contact McCabe?'

Her fingers tightened on the receiver as she sought any hidden meaning in Trevor's question. 'No, Trevor, I don't.' The lie almost lodged in her throat. What would Trevor think if she told him their boss was at that moment in her living-room? She swallowed unsteadily.

Bodie walked past her carefully carrying a tray containing two cups of coffee and a small glass of fruit juice. He disappeared into the living-room, and most of her attention went with him as she tried to hear what was being said in the other room.

'It's just that it's pretty urgent,' Trevor continued. 'I've found some discrepancies in the Nadi accounts. It's been niggling me all week, and I want to make McCabe aware of it before he flies over there. He's leaving on Sunday, isn't he?'

'I'm not sure.' Carolyn tried to concentrate on his words, which was almost impossible since Leith and Bodie seemed to have found a lot to talk about, judging by the murmur of their voices. She began to worry what Bodie might innocently be telling Leith. Not that Bodie knew anything, but——'Have you tried his hotel?' she suggested to Trevor, feeling even more guilty.

'The Crest? Yes, but he's not there.'

'I'm sure if you left a message for him they'd pass it on to him when he returns.' You're a coward, Carolyn Allerton, as well as a mammoth fraud, she admonished herself.

'I guess that's all I can do,' Trevor sighed. 'Well, I won't keep you, Carolyn. Have a good weekend.'

'Yes. Thank you, Trevor.' She hung up thankfully and, adjusting the belt of her robe, rejoined Leith and Bodie.

The coffee stood forgotten on the side table. They had their backs to her and Bodie was holding up one of his cups, explaining to Leith that he'd won it for freestyle earlier in the year. As she stood looking at their two heads together, Bodie so fair, Leith McCabe so dark, she seemed unable to steady her breathing, the pounding of her heart. Leith McCabe had it in his power to upset for ever the even timbre of their lives, hers and Bodie's.

'I'm sorry for the interruption, Mr McCabe,' she said hastily, and they both turned to face her. 'About Fiji——'

Leith held up his hand. 'Bodie explained that he's swimming in an important race on Sunday.' His eyes met hers levelly. 'So we'll change our departure to Monday.'

Carolyn was appalled. 'I can't go, Mr McCabe! I . . . I'm due for annual leave at the end of next week. As I told you, Mr Kruger granted it to me months ago and——'

'And you were intending to be in Melbourne for the Pacific School Games. Bodie told me what an honour it was for him to be chosen to swim for Queensland.'

Carolyn shot a glance at Bodie, wishing he hadn't been quite so forthcoming with so much information.

'Yes, it was,' she agreed weakly. 'So you can see why I'm unable to go to Fiji with you.'

'We'll be finished within the week,' Leith McCabe said easily. 'You can fly back on Friday and leave for Melbourne on Saturday as planned.'

'Simple, Mum,' grinned Bodie. 'Mr McCabe and I worked it all out.'

'But, Bodie, we have to go over to Kedron to collect your uniforms for the Games on Thursday.'

'I can go with Brett and Mrs Conlon. Brett has to get his uniforms, too.' Bodie held out his hands and shrugged. 'No worries, Mum.'

Carolyn gazed impotently at both of them, then Leith was walking across the room towards her. She tensed instinctively, but he only reached for his coffee, lifting it to his lips, taking a sip. Her mind was refusing to function. How was she going to get out of this? Fiji with Leith McCabe would be the height of foolishness. Yet she was tempted——

'What did Mr Green want?' asked Bodie, and Carolyn could almost feel the tension emanating from the other man as he paused, in the act of raising his coffee cup to his lips.

'Actually, he wanted to know where to contact Mr McCabe.' Carolyn made her voice impersonally light, but she knew Leith was watching her. 'Something to do with the Nadi project, he said. I gather it's rather urgent. He left a message at your hotel.'

Leith nodded expressionlessly. 'I'll get back to him.' He held her gaze. 'Thank you.'

'Why didn't you just put Mr McCabe on the phone?' asked Bodie.

'Mr Green was in a hurry,' Carolyn improvised quickly, unable to meet Leith's gaze. 'Now, it's getting late.'

Bodie glanced at his watch. 'Wow. Hadn't you better get dressed, Mum?'

Carolyn's eyes quelled her son and he blinked at her in surprise. His eyes went from his mother to Leith and back again. 'We should be leaving in about ten minutes.' He looked apologetically at Leith. 'It starts at seven and I'm in the first race. Perhaps you'd like to come with us, Mr McCabe?' he asked, and Carolyn could quite cheerfully have throttled him.

'I'm sure Mr McCabe will already have plans for this evening,' she said hurriedly, and unbidden a momentary flash of Leith's smiling face as he talked to the unknown Suzy came back to stab at her in the region of her heart.

'On the contrary,' Leith said easily, 'I'd like to see Bodie in action. I used to do a little competitive swimming myself when I was younger. I'm sure I'd enjoy it.'

Carolyn turned to him in astonishment and she tried to read the expression in his eyes. However, there was no mockery in their blue depths. It seemed he meant what he had said. She swallowed convulsively.

'Hey, that's great, Mr McCabe!' Bodie beamed.

'Perhaps you should get ready, Mrs Allerton,' said Leith, a half-smile now lighting his face and Carolyn could only leave the room to do as he suggested.

She felt completely stunned, as though she had fallen into someone else's crazy dream, that she had to wake herself up to climb back to reality. But part of her didn't want to return to reality, for there she would have to ensure they had nothing more to do with Leith McCabe. And she wanted——Just tonight, she justified, only one night. What could that hurt?

Quickly she stepped into the outfit she had laid out that morning, three-quarter-length pink and white striped pants with a white rope tie belt and a cool pastel pink cotton top that left her arms bare. Slipping her feet into white medium-high sandals, she crossed to her dressing table to apply a little make-up.

Leith and Bodie were still in the living-room and they both stood up as she entered the room. Bodie picked up his sportsbag.

'You look great, Mum,' he smiled at her, his eyes sliding sideways to the other man as though he wanted to be sure Leith had noticed. 'Ready to go?'

Carolyn nodded, making a mental note to have a very meaningful conversation with her son at the earliest opportunity. She resisted the impulse to glance at her boss to see if Bodie's lack of subtlety had gone unnoticed. Some chance, she taunted herself. Leith McCabe never missed a thing.

'We'll take my car,' he said as Carolyn led the way out of the door and down the wide steps.

She paused, about to decline the offer, but Bodie had spotted the Jaguar. He bounded down the path and then stopped to stare.

'Wow. A Jag!' he whistled appreciatively. 'Is it really yours, Mr McCabe?'

'Bodie!' Carolyn admonished him as Leith unlocked the doors.

'Yes, it's mine,' he replied amusedly, holding the door open for her to slip inside.

'Brett will never believe me when I tell him I came in

an XJS!' Bodie scrambled into the back seat and ran his hand over the upholstery. 'He'll think I'm having him on.' He leaned over the front seat between Carolyn and Leith to look at the dash instruments, questioning Leith about their various functions until Carolyn eventually told him to sit back and buckle his seatbelt.

He subsided reluctantly, but kept up a stream of conversation all the way to the swimming venue.

'Bit different from our Gemini, isn't it, Mum?' he said as Leith parked the car and switched off the engine. 'I don't know how Mum's kept it going to and from training and school and work. It wasn't so bad with Mr Kruger, but now that she has to start earlier——' Bodie stopped and gave an embarrassed cough. 'Yes, well, the Gemini's in a pretty bad way,' he finished, and climbed out of the car, opening his mother's door for her, giving her an apologetic grimace.

Carolyn tried to pretend Bodie hadn't put his foot in it, not looking at Leith, smoothing her top over her hips.

'This way, Mr McCabe.' Bodie pointed towards a pathway that disappeared into a mass of native shrubbery.

It was still quite light although dusk wasn't far away and as they left the car a flock of brilliantly coloured rosellas screeched overhead.

'This is nicely set out,' Leith remarked gazing about him at the bottlebrush and gums, the glimpse of a tropical pool through the trees, the gentle tinkle of a creek flowing beneath the walkway bridge they were crossing.

'The pool's the best, too,' Bodie boasted cheerfully as they moved out of the trees and up the path to the building itself.

Inside there seemed to be people everywhere, officials, swimmers, the public. With the ease of someone who is at home in the large complex Bodie led them through to the stands of seats.

'I'll have to go straight down,' he said. 'Will you be

sitting in your usual place, Mum?'

Carolyn nodded, still very much aware of the tall man beside her.

'Good luck, Bodie,' said Leith.

'Yes, good luck, love,' she said softly, putting her arm around Bodie's shoulders and giving him a squeeze.

'Thanks, Mum.' Bodie planted a quick noisy kiss on her cheek and with a wave, hurried off to join his fellow competitors.

'We'll go up one flight,' she said breathily. 'We find you get a better view from there.' She started up the stairs, the hair on the back of her neck prickling as she felt him close behind her. As they reached the top of the steps Brett Conlon's mother waved to her, indicating she had kept some spare seats. A little reluctantly Carolyn crossed to where the Conlons and a few of the other swimmers' parents were sitting. A dull flush brushed her cheeks as Joy Conlon's eyes went from Carolyn to the tall man beside her and mentally she prepared herself for Joy's questions she knew would come later. She made the introductions and then fortunately someone else claimed Joy's attention.

Suppressing a sigh of relief, Carolyn sat down, wishing there were more room on the benchlike seat, as Leith sat next to her, his sleeve brushing her bare arm, his trouser-clad thigh resting against her. Her skin burned where her body touched his. Could he feel it, too?

She slid a sideways glance at him, only to find his eyes on her, deep blue and unfathomable. Nervously she began to explain the scene to him, pointing out the warm-up pool, the way the main pool was designed to minimise turbulence in the outside lanes.

Her gaze was drawn irresistibly to him again and her eyes met his, her voice faltering and dying. Her mouth had gone dry and her heartbeats swelled in her chest. Leith was the first to break the tense silence and she couldn't wrench her eyes from his.

'I didn't know you had a son.'

Carolyn's tongue tip came out to moisten her lips. 'How old is he?'

'Just . . . just thirteen,' she got out. This was dreadful. She had to stop his questions. But how?

'What happened to his father?'

She swallowed achingly. 'He . . . he died,' she told him huskily, 'before Bodie was born.'

'And you failed to mention that you had an arrangement with John Kruger to begin work at nine instead of eight-thirty. Why didn't you tell me?'

'You didn't exactly give me a chance,' she replied quietly, not looking at him, and his fingers took hold of her chin, gently lifting her face until their eyes met.

'Was I such an ogre?' His voice dropped, deeply liquid, an exquisite torture.

'No, but——' Carolyn swallowed breathlessly, trying to draw her crumbling defences into some order. In the crowd of people, the talking, the laughing, they were alone, wrapped in an excitant cocoon. 'But we've . . . I've . . . Joy and I have rearranged our schedules so . . .' Her voice gave out on her and she could only continue to drown in his eyes.

And she was drowning. Leith held her gaze, a small nerve pulsing at the corner of his mouth. He caught a ragged breath and released her, his eyes going back to the scene below them, the activity, the cool turquoise water, the faint aroma of chlorine.

'You must have had a hard time raising a child on your own,' he said, his voice still a little raw.

'No,' Carolyn shook her head, 'not really. My aunt was alive when he was small and she gave me great support.' She'd recovered part of her composure now and a faint smile touched the corners of her mouth. 'Besides, if all children were like Bodie, everyone would have half a dozen!'

Leith smiled then, too, and she felt the tight knot of tension in her stomach begin to relax.

'Not that I'm prejudiced.' Her smile widened.

'Of course not,' he agreed easily.

Carolyn used the opportunity to study him. He had a classically masculine profile, well defined, hard and rugged. Apart from his lips. The sensual curve of them had a spiral of warmth radiating upwards inside her, bringing the flush back to her cheeks as the timbre of her inner tension changed. Nervous uncertainty gave way to a far more basically sexual tautness and she yearned to reach out her hand, slide her fingers over the firm hard muscles of his thigh resting so close to her own.

He turned back to her then, catching her watching him, and for a split second she saw her own awareness reflected in his eyes before the shutters fell.

'And Green, where does he fit in?' he asked with a quiet harshness that reached only her ears.

'Trevor?' Carolyn's voice wavered at the shock of his question. Her thought processes spun crazily and in those few seconds a tiny voice inside her made the most of her dazed hesitation.

Tell him Trevor's more than a friend, tell him you're committed to Trevor. Use him as camouflage to put Leith McCabe off. Nip the rising awareness they both knew existed between them in the bud, before it went any further, before she was in too deep to get out.

Carolyn shrugged. 'Just a work associate,' she heard herself say.

'Why didn't you simply hand the phone over to me when he called?'

His question took her totally unawares and before she could formulate an answer he spoke again.

'Have you always guarded your private life so zealously?'

She swallowed. 'I suppose I have. I just thought perhaps you'd prefer not to——' Her voice gave out on her.

Leith held her gaze for a long moment and then he nodded, an expression on his face that filled Carolyn with a sudden horror. No, Leith, there's no future in it.

There can never be anything between us.

'Mr McCabe, I——' she began agitatedly.

'Call me Leith, Carolyn,' he said easily, his hand reaching up to loosen his tie, pulling it off and slipping it into the pocket of his jacket. He undid the top buttons of his shirt and sat back in his seat, seemingly perfectly at ease.

'How does Bodie expect to fare in his races this evening?' he asked, and Carolyn pulled her scattered, shattered thoughts together to answer him.

Surprisingly the evening flew by. Bodie won a gold medallion in his two hundred metres backstroke event and a silver in the four hundred metres individual medley. Bodie's coach came up while he was changing into his tracksuit and in his typically outrageous fashion wrapped his arms around Carolyn and kissed her on the cheek.

'What did you think of our boy tonight, Carrie? What did I tell you? He's a natural. He has Commonwealth and Olympic gold written all over him, in every stroke he takes!' He sobered. 'And no one deserves it more than he does. Or his beautiful mother.' He gave her another squeeze and ran back down the stairs.

Carolyn coughed a little embarrassedly. 'He's . . . Bodie's coach is very enthusiastic,' she started to explain.

'So I see,' Leith remarked drily as Bodie rejoined them. He was ecstatic about receiving his medallions and as they drove home he jangled them together.

'Coach says he's realy proud of me, especially for the medley one. Butterfly's my weakest stroke,' he explained to Leith, 'and I bettered my time for it by a whole second. I can't even believe it myself!'

They pulled up at the house and Bodie sprang out to open the door for his mother.

'Thanks for taking us, Mr McCabe,' he held out his hand and Leith shook it. 'It's a fabulous car, it really is.'

'Thanks, Bodie.' In the bright moonlight Carolyn saw the flash of his white teeth as he smiled. 'I thoroughly enjoyed the evening and watching you swim. You did well. And good luck for Sunday.'

'Thanks, Mr McCabe.'

'Do you think I might talk to your mother for a moment?' asked Leith.

'Oh, sure.' Bodie beamed at them both, gave a soft chuckle and walked up the path to the steps.

Carolyn decided the sooner she talked to Bodie, the better. He had obviously read more into Leith's interest than was there, and that sort of complication she could do without.

'We'll leave for Fiji after lunch Monday,' Leith was saying, 'so don't worry about coming in to the office until around ten.'

'But the flight may be booked out,' Carolyn began.

'I'll be taking the company jet,' he replied, as though it were an everyday means of getting from one place to another. But then for Leith it was, Carolyn reflected with resignation. 'Any more word on your car?'

'No. But I can't see it being ready before we leave.' She frowned. 'Perhaps Trevor could collect it for me.'

'I'll see to it,' he said firmly.

'Oh, but I can't let you——'

'Carolyn, leave it with me. I'll have it delivered to the car pool. They can garage it there until you come back from Fiji.'

'All right,' she agreed reluctantly, and thought she heard him give a soft laugh.

'Don't tell me you're giving in without a fight?' he asked lightly. 'I don't believe it. You're one of the most stubbornly independent women I've met.'

It has always been safer that way, Carolyn went to tell him, but she remained silent, not wanting to analyse the rush of pleasure it gave her to relinquish a decision to someone else. Four fourteen years she had been virtually on her own, making her own decisions. Her aunt had always insisted that Carolyn stood on her own two feet. If a girl was old enough to have a child, her aunt maintained, she was old enough to be responsible for herself and her baby.

The silence was stretching between them and Carolyn felt that same tension clutch at her, reach out to enfold her.

'It does seem to be the simplest solution,' she agreed hurriedly, and could feel he was smiling.

'I think so,' he said evenly. 'No trouble leaving Bodie with the Conlons?'

'No.' She shook her head. 'I'm sure there won't be. Their son, Brett, often stays with us, so it always works out marvellously well.'

'Good.' He sighed and ran his hand around the back of his neck, making Carolyn realise he must be tired. He'd flown up north and back again, driven from the airport to the office and then out here to spend an evening in the midst of a cheering crowd. 'I would have liked to come along and watch Bodie in his eight hundred metres on Sunday,' he was saying, 'but unfortunately I have commitments all weekend. Getting away to leave for Fiji on Sunday as I originally planned was going to take some precision timing. Now that we're leaving on Monday I can relax a little over the Sunday meeting. Wish Bodie good luck for me.'

'Thank you, I will.' Carolyn took a step backwards as Leith closed her door.

He turned to look towards the house. 'He's a fine boy,' he said softly as he moved around the front of the car. 'I'll see you on Monday.' He opened the driver's side door and paused before climbing inside. 'And Carolyn, not before ten.'

She nodded. 'Thank you.' She made no attempt to walk up to the house until he had driven away, and when she did the sound of his deep voice saying her name was still playing down the sensitive nerve-endings of her spine.

Bodie was waiting for her in the kitchen, just adding

milk to the cup of tea he had made her. He looked up with a smile.

'What a beaut night!' He sighed. 'The best night I've ever had. Wasn't it great, Mum?'

Carolyn picked up his two medallions from the table and smiled back at him. 'Great. I don't remember seeing you swim as well.'

'Not just that, Mum. I mean the whole evening, meeting Mr McCabe, riding in his fantastic car, and—well, everything.' Bodie passed her her mug of tea. 'And isn't it fabulous you're going to Fiji?'

'I'd prefer it if it weren't the week before your Pacific School Games,' Carolyn replied lightly, taking a sip of her tea and leading the way through to the living-room.

'That's no problem, Mum.' Bodie sat down opposite her. 'I'll be fine with the Conlons. I just want you to not worry about anything and to have a good time.'

'I'll be working, Bodie, from daylight till dusk if Mr McCabe's running true to form.' She grimaced, and Bodie smiled.

'I like him.'

Carolyn slid a glance at him and murmured noncommittally.

'He's nice, and I think he likes you, Mum.'

'Bodie.' She set her tea down on the coffee table and frowned at her son.

He held up his hand. 'Okay, okay. But he does like you. I can tell.'

With that he stood up and crossed to the bookshelf, taking down a photograph album, flipping the pages until he found the one he wanted. His young face was serious in profile and Carolyn walked over to join him, her eyes going to the open page and the two not-quite-sharp coloured photographs.

One showed a group of seven teenagers leaning nonchalantly over three motor-cycles. The other photograph was a little more posed, a shot of a tall youth astride a motor-bike.

Carolyn felt her throat tighten as she studied the young faces in the group, finding the thin defiant adolescent that had been herself at sixteen. She wore skin-tight denims, a T-shirt that moulded her young breasts, and one finger draped a matching denim jacket over her shoulder. Her hair was fair, not long and not short, and it sprang out in its natural waves, wild and untamed as she had been. To Carolyn that figure looked so youthfully vulnerable, a little tough hiding a multitude of fears and angry hostilities. When the photo was taken she had been unaware of her pregnancy.

Her eyes skimmed the other photo, settling on the dark hair, the slightly mutinous boyish good looks. A real heart-throb, the other girls had called him. Carolyn searched the fuzzy print for some spark she could hold on to, to put some life into Bodie's father. But it escaped her. It was just a photo of a boy, for he was only four years older than Bodie was now. Just a typical teenager, long darkish hair, dressed in the usual denim uniform, legs astride a motor-cycle that looked too much for him to handle.

'We've never talked about him much, have we?' Bodie said softly.

'No, I suppose we haven't,' she agreed, her voice low and husky.

She heard him sigh softly. 'I guess you must have loved him a lot, hey?' he said quietly, his voice recently deepening in tone catching in his throat, and he swallowed. 'My dad, I mean,' he explained needlessly.

The breath seemed to have been drawn from Carolyn's body and a pain clutched at her heart. Oh, Bodie. If only I could—If you only knew that's the hardest question to answer that you've ever asked me. Why couldn't it be that straightforward?

She reached out and put her hand on his shoulder and his eyes met hers.

'I mean, you've never been interested in anyone else all

these years, so you must have loved him heaps,' Bodie elaborated.

What was she going to say to him? Was it the right time to tell him all of it, the whole dreadful truth, instead of the half-truth she had rehearsed so often she had almost begun to believe it herself? Until Leith McCabe had appeared before her, that was, bringing every last detail back with brutal clarity.

'It was all such a long time ago, Bodie,' she heard herself say. 'I was very young and he—your father—wasn't much older. We were both far too young to have the responsibility of a baby.' She paused painfully. 'If I were honest I'd say I hardly knew him. Oh, I don't mean I'd just met him. We'd known each other at school. But——' She stopped and shrugged.

Bodie's grey eyes watched her thoughtfully and then he looked back at the photograph. 'Was he a nice guy?'

'He was nice to me,' Carolyn said carefully. And in his way, he had been, understanding her desire to escape from a home situation she found intolerable. 'I used to think he was very brave and tough. He was the leader of our group and we all looked up to him.'

Bodie nodded.

'If he hadn't died before you were born things would have been different, but I'm sure of one thing, love,' she drew him against her, hugging him, 'he would have been as proud of you as I am.'

Bodie's face flushed and he cleared his throat. 'Thanks, Mum.' He closed the album, returned it to the shelf, and they sat down again. Bodie rested his elbows on his knees and regarded her seriously. 'I really do like Mr McCabe, Mum. You know, I reckon you should marry him.'

Carolyn opened her mouth and closed it again, unable to utter a sound.

'Don't you think it's a good idea?' Bodie continued. 'I mean, it would solve all our problems.'

'What problems?' she croaked.

'Well,' he frowned, 'financial ones. Our car, for instance. Mr McCabe would fix it up, I'll bet. And we wouldn't have to worry about saving so hard for the Commonwealth Games and the Olympics or my training fees. He must be pretty rich, having a car like the Jag.'

'Bodie, that's being dreadfully mercenary and you know it! We manage quite well and I will get the car fixed after Christmas.'

'I just want things to be easier for you. And if you got married I'd know there was someone to take care of you while I'm away.' Bodie persevered, undaunted.

'Away where?' Carolyn demanded.

He shrugged. 'When I go away with the team. Coach is talking about Singapore and maybe Canada. If you couldn't get time off work you'd be here alone.'

'Bodie, I can manage on my own,' Carolyn began angrily, standing up and crossing to the window.

'I've upset you, haven't I?' He walked up behind her, his young face worried. 'I didn't mean to, Mum.'

Carolyn put her arms around him and hugged him. 'I know you didn't,' she sighed. 'Things aren't nearly as simple as that, love. I can't marry someone just because he can afford to pay our way, don't you see that?'

Bodie nodded reluctantly. 'I guess. You'd have to love him like you did my dad.'

'Yes, I'd have to love him,' she said softly, trying to bring his father's face into her mind but finding her memory letting her down. The hard craggy face of Leith McCabe had somehow eclipsed those other boyish features. 'And I'd have to feel my marriage was right for you,' she added, giving him a quick squeeze as he went to interrupt. 'Now, enough of this. Come on, we'd best get to bed. It's late, and you have two more events tomorrow.'

They walked along the hall to the bedrooms, Carolyn switching off the lights as they went. When they reached her room Bodie turned and kissed her on the cheek.

'Night, Mum.' He turned away and then stopped,

looking seriously back at his mother. 'But if you did kind of decide you were in love with Mr McCabe, and he wanted to marry you, you would, wouldn't you?'

'Bodie, please!' Carolyn began exasperatedly.

'Okay.' He expelled a heavy breath. 'But just remember, it's fine with me.'

Carolyn lay in bed and ran a slightly shaky hand over her eyes. Looking at the old photographs again had unsettled her, brought memories of that fateful time knocking on the door to her consciousness. The past tugged at the present, crying for release, but she kept that door firmly closed. She didn't want to remember. Not tonight.

As far as Bodie knew his father had been accidentally killed six months before he was born. Strangely, he had never been over-curious, content with the unembellished basic facts she had told him.

She always knew that some day she'd have to tell him more, at least more than he knew now. She swallowed agitatedly. He was thirteen, growing up so fast, and she had been expecting him to ask for more details. But he hadn't. And no matter how often she tossed it over in her mind she had never found the words to explain it, to tell him everything, not without going into the tragedy, the horror, or her part in that needless waste of young lives.

And Leith knew it all, every last dreadful detail that had been made so painfully public at the trial. No. No. The inquest. It had been an inquest, not a trial.

Oh, Bodie, what should I do? Her heart ached. Bodie meant more to her than life itself, had been her whole life until . . . She paused, but couldn't push the thought out of her mind. Until Leith McCabe had re-entered her life.

As she drifted into a troubled sleep it was of Leith that she was thinking. Of his fingers on her chin, and of the burning fire in his eyes.

CHAPTER SIX

LEITH sat back in his chair stretching his arms above his head, flexing his tired muscles.

'We'll call it a day, I think.' He glanced at his wristwatch. 'I might go down to the pool for a swim before I get ready for dinner. How about you?'

Carolyn's eyes went to the notes she had to type, and he frowned.

'Leave those until the morning.'

'I could have them half finished if I started now,' she began, but Leith stood up, taking her notebook from her hands, closing it and setting it on to the desk.

'I hereby decree that the office is closed as of now,' he smiled crookedly. 'Boss's orders, Carolyn. Take some time to relax. Didn't you say everyone needs a break at some time?' He raised one dark eyebrow. 'Come swimming or go down to the spa,' he suggested.

'Well, I do have a couple of postcards to write,' she said, and his mouth quirked.

'Postcards? Sure I can't tempt you into a swim?'

Carolyn shook her head. Swimming with Leith would be an exquisite form of torture and she was afraid to allow herself to indulge in it.

'Okay, if I can't talk you into it I'll see you back here about seven.' He strode across to his room with long easy strides.

Carolyn waited until the door had closed behind him before gathering up her notes and the dossier they had been working on and sliding them into the drawer of her desk. She locked the drawer, frowning slightly as she recalled returning to the room just after lunch on their first day in Fiji to find Peter Kruger leafing through the

file. Since then she'd been careful to lock everything away.

By the time they'd arrived here on Monday it was growing dark, so they had seen little of the countryside in their taxi journey to the hotel. Leith had reserved a large suite on the top floor and it consisted of a large sitting-room where they had set up an office, and two luxurious bedrooms, each with its own bathroom.

Never had Carolyn seen such quietly tasteful magnificence, and the view from her bedroom balcony the next morning with its lush tropical foliage of variegated greenery to the almost painful blue of the ocean in the distance had very nearly taken her breath away.

From the sitting-room balcony they could see the huge hotel and shopping complex Kruger's was building. It had a prime position and Carolyn knew that the architectural design was outstanding. But the project was way beyond schedule and each day cost Kruger's, and now NatCon, a great deal of money.

Immediately after an early breakfast that first day they were in the car Leith had hired and were heading over to the company's construction site. By the time Peter Kruger arrived Leith had made a thorough inspection of the whole project and it was clear that he was not impressed.

Peter Kruger's excuses were mainly based on the inconsistency of the local work-force, but it was obvious that he hadn't an ounce of rapport with any of the foremen they spoke to as Leith allowed Peter to escort them over the ground they had already covered. By the time Leith and Carolyn returned to the hotel for lunch Carolyn could feel the suppressed anger in every line of Leith's body.

'I'm going to get one of my men, Joe Dawson, over to clear up this fiasco,' he said as he drove back to their hotel. 'He's already had experience with construction in Fiji as well as a couple of other Pacific islands. Has Kruger always been this incompetent?'

Carolyn shrugged. 'He's never had the reins on a project this size until now. Previously his father's had advisers with him.'

Leith expelled an uncomplimentary exclamation. 'From what I saw he's just bone lazy and this project can't afford to carry anyone, even Peter Kruger. He can work with Joe and he'll learn or he's out. Peter Kruger is due for some hard facts when he turns up this afternoon.'

And after lunch Carolyn was on her own in the suite when Peter Kruger arrived. She had slipped into her room to freshen up and when she re-entered the living-room she found Peter peering at Leith's personal files. She walked straight across to the desk, forcing him to step aside.

'How did you get in here?' she asked him, purposefully closing the file. Somehow she didn't think Leith would care to have Peter Kruger going over his confidential information.

'The maid.' Peter smiled unabashed.

'Were you wanting something specific?' She attempted to control her anger and he laughed harshly.

'Still the cold unbending keeper of the office, Carolyn?' he'd queried, with a smile that didn't reach his eyes. 'You always guarded Dad like that, too. Although it must be a change working for someone as young and dynamic as the new boss.'

To her annoyance a tinge of colour washed over Carolyn's cheeks, and Peter didn't miss it.

'Well, well, has some of the ice melted?' Peter laughed snidely. 'Careful you don't get burned, Carolyn. I hear he has something of a long list of discarded beauties scattered behind him.'

'Don't be ridiculous,' she retorted shortly. She had disliked Peter Kruger on sight and in the nine years she had worked for his father's firm he had never given her any reason to revise that instant antipathy.

He crossed to stand close beside her, his hand reaching out to trail down her bare arm. 'You know, I've always wondered whether that cold calmness wasn't a veneer covering a molten centre. Is it, Carolyn?'

She drew back, barely hiding her revulsion, and his lips twisted nastily.

'Did you know my father made it pretty clear to me he was very much in favour of having you as a daughter-in-law?'

Carolyn's gaze swung to him in surprise.

'Oh, yes, he was all for it, but you wouldn't even look at me, would you, Mrs Persil White? Always looking down your nose at me, making me feel I wasn't good enough for you!'

'Peter, I——'

His bitter laugh cut her off. 'Maybe I should show you what you've been missing.'

His arms were around her before she could move and his lips claimed hers with hard brutality. Carolyn struggled against the tight bands that held her and she felt a rising nausea as his lips forced hers apart. Her strength was no match for his, and in desperation she lifted her foot and kicked him hard on his shin. His gasp of pain caused him momentarily to slacken his hold on her and she broke away, putting the desk between them.

Peter swore profusely and reached down to rub his bruised leg. 'That hurt, Carolyn!' he snapped angrily.

'It was meant to hurt!' she threw back at him. 'Don't ever touch me again!'

'Oh, I won't. I've found out what I wanted to know,' he mocked. 'You're pure ice right through. No man wants to get frostbite when he kisses a woman. You're frigid, Carolyn. I wonder if that kid you've got is actually yours!'

Carolyn's hand itched to slap his petulant face. 'I'd appreciate it if you waited outside for Mr McCabe,' she said in a clipped voice, and he laughed harshly again.

'You know, if you want to catch McCabe's eye you'll have to thaw a bit. A man like McCabe can take his pick of the young lovelies. He won't have the time or the patience to chip through the ice.'

'Get out.' Carolyn's throat closed in her anger.

'Or has he already discovered your little problem for himself?' Peter jeered, and sat down in a comfortable chair. 'I'll wait for McCabe.'

Before Carolyn could comment Leith entered the suite and she thankfully escaped to her room leaving the two men together.

When Leith left for his swim she settled down on the comfortable lounger on her own balcony and she slipped off her shoes, stretching out her feet. Hmm! It felt good to relax, and she welcomed this time to herself. She desperately needed an hour or so to recharge her batteries, strengthen her defences against the distracting, heady proximity of Leith McCabe.

The whole trip, these past three days, had been a time of alternating exhilaration and despair, and totally exhausting. She delighted in being with him, but she was also weighed down with the heavy regret that she could never allow herself to be any more than his very impersonal secretary. Having him so close to her was a bittersweet pleasure.

And she knew he watched her. She continually felt his gaze moving over her and it took all her willpower not to raise her eyes to his, let him see the yearning invitation she suspected she would be incapable of disguising.

With a sigh Carolyn reached for her pen and jotted off a postcard to Bodie. Although she knew he probably wouldn't receive it until they returned from Melbourne he could add the stamp to his collection.

She glanced at her watch. It was too early to ring him, he would still be at training. She would have to do that when she returned to the suite after dinner, hoping they weren't too late back.

She wasn't really in the mood for the dinner party Leith had arranged for this evening, but he had taken it for granted she would attend. With his usual arrogance, she reflected ungraciously, then felt a trifle guilty. She was here to work and tonight was part of her job, so why should her boss not expect her to be on hand? It was a business dinner anyway.

Fortunately there would only be three other couples besides herself and Leith. She groaned softly. She would be glad when this week was over. Keeping a calm impersonal front when she was with Leith was wearing her down. At least back in Brisbane he had other business to attend to that kept him out of the office.

Standing reluctantly, she left the balcony and showered before getting ready for dinner. The dress she chose to wear was a neat black sheath, elegantly simple in style and cut, a dress suitable for most occasions. Carolyn refused to think how many years she had had it, for the design didn't date fashionwise. The low neckline and thin shoulder straps showed off the soft glow of her even tan and the narrow belted waist emphasised her figure to perfection.

Carefully she applied a little light make-up, concentrating mainly on her eyes, then went to wind her hair up into its usual chignon. Something made her pause, take in the softness of the waving fall of her fair hair curling silkily on to her bare shoulders. She shivered slightly. It made her look younger, less austere, and for a moment she was tempted to leave it down. Her eyes ran over her reflection again and she saw the vulnerability there in her eyes, the line of her mouth, and shook her head exasperatedly, deftly pulling her hair up into its usual style.

Right on seven she slipped on her high-heeled sandals and left her room. When she entered the sitting-room Leith was standing by the sliding glass doors, his body in profile as he gazed out into the falling night. He held a glass of his favourite Scotch in his hand, and as Carolyn watched he raised the glass absently to his lips, taking a sip. She followed his movements, her chest suddenly tight with the physical pain of preventing herself from rushing over to him, wrapping her arms around him, pressing her lips to the smooth strong line of his jaw.

He glanced down at the amber liquid in his glass and grimaced, swallowing the remainder of his drink in barely restrained irritation. What could have upset him? Carolyn reflected as he turned, catching sight of her as she made herself move forward.

His eyes ran over her, setting her heartbeats skipping erratically and she could see the tension in the line of his jaw, the way he held his whole body. Carolyn was unable to prevent her own eyes from drinking in every facet of him. He was so magnetic, so potently attractive that just looking at him sent a wave of yearning twisting inside her. He was wearing a light grey suit cut impeccably to the broad muscular lines of his body and the pale blue of his shirt only drew attention to the colour of his eyes, now burning with a deep brilliance that was reaching out to inflame her.

'Would you like a drink before we go down?' he asked evenly, the very impersonality of his tone dousing the fire in her, replacing the warmth with a cold numbness.

She shook her head. 'No, thank you.' Her voice came out thinly and she turned away from him in case he saw the pain reflected in her grey eyes.

'Then shall we go?' He replaced his glass on the bar-top with a restrained clink and they crossed to the door, Leith holding it open for her and following her into the hallway and along to the elevator.

She was aware of his every stride on the sound-muffling carpet, every nuance of movement in his long lithe body. And inside the elevator it was worse, the tension between them so thick Carolyn felt she could taste it.

She couldn't stop herself slanting a glance at him, but he gave nothing away, his face set, his eyes on the illuminated numbers of the floors they passed as they slid downwards.

The restaurant was beautifully decorated in fine tropical style with lots of cool fernery and palms and colourfully dressed waiters and waitresses. Leith had reserved a table and Carolyn knew he expected her to take in everything that was said over dinner, so she forced herself to regain some semblance of calmness.

Joe and Pam Dawson, who had arrived from Melbourne the evening before, were waiting for them in the small bar that overlooked the dining-room. The four of them sat chatting until the other two couples joined them. The men were Fijian and both were foremen on the Kruger Project, one in his late thirties and the other in his mid-twenties. Their wives were shyly quiet, both beautiful girls with liquid brown eyes and smooth dark skin.

Surprisingly the dinner was a huge success, due in the main, Carolyn had to admit, to Leith's expertise at putting everyone at their ease. Everyone except Carolyn. Her tension only grew as she sat opposite her boss more totally aware of him than she'd been of any other man in her whole life.

With the meal behind them the two Fijian couples took to the dance-floor, leaving Leith and Joe deep in a discussion about a new type of building material.

Pam raised her eyebrows exasperatedly, and tapped her husband on the arm. 'They're playing our song, Joe.' She took her husband's arm when he stood up as his wife and Carolyn rejoined them. With a goodnatured grumble he crossed to the dance-floor with her, leaving Carolyn to sit down a little breathlessly, alone now with Leith McCabe.

'The evening has gone well,' she ventured nervously when she could stand the widening silence no longer.

'Yes.' Leith dragged his gaze from his contemplation of his coffee-cup.

'Shall I type up a report in the morning?'

He turned to look at her, his expression veiled. 'No, I don't think so. We'll put this down to public relations.'

She wondered if she imagined the wry twist to his lips. 'All right.' She swallowed, wishing she could just excuse herself and leave. She glanced surreptitiously at her wristwatch. If she didn't call Bodie within the next half-hour she would be too late, because he'd be in bed.

'Shall we dance?' Leith asked flatly, standing up and indicating she should do the same before she had time to refuse.

His words had taken her by surprise and involuntarily she got to her feet. 'Oh, look, it doesn't matter. We don't have to dance if you'd rather not,' she stammered, to no avail, for he took her arm and led her on to the dance-floor, his arms going around her, holding her loosely, impersonally.

Carolyn's breath caught in her throat as one of her hands was clasped in his and his arm lightly encircled her waist. She rested her other hand hesitantly on his broad shoulder and the warm male scent of him teased her, made her yearn to be held closer. Her feet followed his lead automatically, for she felt too bemused to guide them. This close Leith McCabe was devastating.

'Relax, Carolyn,' he said a little curtly, and she glanced up at him, startled by the tone in his voice.

His jaw was set, his lips tight and unsmiling, and he didn't look as though he was enjoying himself. Carolyn caught her bottom lip with her teeth. She hadn't asked him to dance with her, had she?

'We can sit down if you'd rather, Mr McCabe,' she began. 'I realise I'm here to work and—well, I don't want you to feel——.' She stopped at the coldness in his piercing blue eyes. 'That you have to dance with me,' she finished lamely, her voice thick and husky.

He was still looking down at her, his eyelids shielding the expression in his eyes, but she could feel the tension in his body now.

'What makes you think I ever do anything I don't want to do?' he asked then, and she saw the throb of a tiny pulsebeat at the corner of his mouth. 'And I thought we'd decided you'd call me Leith. Didn't we, Carolyn?'

She nodded, swallowing as her heartbeats reacted to the liquid tone he used to say her name. 'Yes. But I thought as it's a business evening . . .' Her voice faded away.

'We must keep everything strictly businesslike,' he finished mockingly. 'Are you always so proper, Mrs Allerton?'

She was incapable of answering. The tension between them was so emotion-charged she knew it was about to rage out of control.

'Do you ever——?' He stopped, his eyes surveying her broodingly, then his lips thinned. 'No matter. Would you like to sit down?' His face was set and closed and she could only nod and accompany him on shaky legs back to their table.

The older couple of Leith's Fijian guests were sitting sipping their coffee and when Leith made to hold Carolyn's chair for her she took advantage of the moment to make her escape.

'I think I might call it a night if I may. I'm feeling a little tired.' She glanced uncertainly at him and he inclined his head, his face devoid of expression. She could barely stifle her sigh of relief as she thankfully said her goodbyes to the Fijian couple, asked Leith to make her apologies to the others and fled. It cost her dear to walk evenly across to the door of the restaurant, for her feet wanted to race, as though she had the devil himself in pursuit.

Back in her room Carolyn sank down on her bed, her fingers gently massaging her temples, her body weak now from her prolonged tension. She groaned softly. How she had wanted to sway in his arms for ever, rest her head against his broad shoulder, move her fingers in his dark hair, feel his body——

She sprang off the bed, her hands clasped together to still their trembling. If only——If only nothing, she told herself brutally. You can't allow this to go any further and you know it. It's impossible. There's no way he could ever overlook what he thinks you've done, so you'd sooner try to grasp the stars.

Slowly she kicked off her shoes, slipped out of her dress and her gossamer nylons and donned her short terry-towelling robe. Leith should be tied up for some time yet, so she would call Bodie and be in bed before he returned.

On bare feet she left her room and crossed to the telephone. Making the connection took longer than she thought it should, and she sighed testily as a series of clicks changed to a distant ringing tone. Then Joy Conlon's voice came on the line echoing flatly.

'Carolyn!' she squealed. 'How's Fiji, you lucky duck?'

'It's great,' Carolyn smiled, 'although I've been working flat out.'

'Now, Carolyn, that gorgeous man couldn't possibly be a slavedriver,' Joy teased.

'Oh, couldn't he?' said Carolyn with feeling, and Joy laughed. 'Is everything going okay?'

'Everything's fine,' Joy assured her. 'And I take it by everything you mean Bodie. He's here hanging over my shoulder, so I'll put him on. See you, Carolyn.'

'Yes. 'Bye, Joy.'

'Mum!' The sound of Bodie's voice brought a lump to Carolyn's throat. 'How've you been?'

'Fine, love. How are you?'

'No worries,' Bodie said easily. 'We're going over to get our uniforms and have our photos taken tomorrow for the School Games.'

'How's your training coming?'

'Just great, Mum.' Bodie's voice was full of enthusiasm. 'Coach's really pleased with me, especially since my win in the eight hundred on Sunday. I'm going so well I reckon I'll stand a chance in Melbourne next week. I can hardly wait!'

A noise behind Carolyn had her swinging around, her knuckles turning white where she clutched the receiver as Leith closed the door behind him, pocketing his keys and moving lithely towards her. He threw his jacket on a chair and began undoing his tie, his eyes meeting hers across the room.

'To swim and to see you, Mum.' Bodie's voice drew her attention back to the phone and she turned away from Leith's probing gaze. 'Are you enjoying Fiji?'

'Yes.' Her voice broke nervously and she drew a tortured breath. 'It's a little different from what I imagined, but it's lovely.'

'That's good. Is Mr McCabe enjoying it, too?'

'Yes, but we've been working fairly hard,' she answered cautiously, aware of Leith crossing to the bar, hearing the splash of liquid in a glass.

'I miss you, Mum.' Bodie's serious voice brought a rush of tears to her eyes.

'I miss you, too, love,' she said thickly.

'But I guess it won't be long till Friday, only two more days.'

'Mmm. I'm looking forward to it, too.' Carolyn swallowed painfully. 'Well, I'd better go, love. I'm glad everything's going well. Keep training hard.'

'I will. Say hello to Mr McCabe for me. See you soon, Mum. 'Bye!' Bodie made a sloppy kissing noise and laughed. ' 'Bye, love.' Carolyn slowly replaced the receiver and suddenly her tears overflowed, ran coursing down her cheeks. She groped unsuccessfully in the pockets of her robe for a tissue.

A snowy-white handkerchief was thrust into her hand and she spun around, raising tear-filled eyes to gaze up at him. His face swam mistily and she blinked, trying to focus. She wiped her eyes, so aware of the musky fragrance of him that lingered on the still-warm material.

'I'm sorry,' she whispered hoarsely, and another tear trickled down her cheek. 'Bodie said to say hello to you.'

He raised his hand, catching the tear on his finger, gazing down at it with eyes now a brilliant indigo blue, the colour of the deep unfathomable ocean. Time stood perfectly still and Carolyn knew she couldn't even be breathing. The moment grew explosively emotion-charged, gathering impetus until she heard him groan softly, deep in his throat, and his arms went around her, propelling her to him so that her cheek rested against his chest, registering the heavy acceleration of his heartbeats.

CHAPTER SEVEN

AND hers raced in unison. She could feel the long solid length of him moulded to her and her mouth went dry with the wave of physical longing that rose inside her. She turned her head and pressed her lips to the warmth of his chest. Of their own accord her arms slid around him, her fingertips delighting in the feel of the hard muscles beneath the thin silk of his shirt.

They strained together, bodies arching, desperately seeking the ultimate closeness in a timeless thought-destroying wonder. Leith's lips rained soft ecstatic kisses on her temple, over her eyes, along her jaw.

'Carolyn—Carolyn,' he murmured thickly. 'Do you realise just how long I've wanted to hold you like this, feel your body close to mine, wanted to caress you, kiss——' His last words were lost in her mouth as his lips claimed hers, plundering, besieging, demanding a response Carolyn gave spontaneously, all past and future erased from her mind. There was only now, with Leith's body joined to hers, his lips possessing hers. And their passion rose, like a bushfire raging way out of control, and neither of them attempted to stop it.

Leith's fingers found the pins in her hair, pulling them out, letting it fall freely in silken cascades. He threaded it around his fingers, lifting it so that he could drink in its clear fragrance.

'Don't put it up. It's a sin to confine it like that. From the moment I saw you I've wanted to take it down.' His tone was deep and rawly husky, and Carolyn shivered, her nerve-ends tingling delightedly.

His lips found her ear, gently nibbling her lobe, trailed downwards to the curve of her neck, his fingers pushing aside her robe, his mouth sliding sensuously over her bare shoulder. One hand moved around her ribcage to envelop her full breast and a wave of such pure desire had her wondering if her knees would give way beneath her. Gently caressing, his thumb found her taut nipple through the thin lace of her bra. He undid the clasp, setting her breasts free, letting his fingers encircle her naked flesh, and she moaned deep in her throat, her body far past any thought of resistance arching invitingly towards him.

And he was as aroused as she was, she could not mistake that, and she exulted in his surging response.

Leith leant back a little, his breath catching in his throat as he gazed down at her breasts.

'Beautiful,' he murmured. 'So beautiful. I wanted to see you like this before we went down to dinner, to hold you, caress you. I knew all afternoon I wouldn't want to share one moment with you with anyone else.'

She saw the passion in the softened lines of his face,the sensual curve of his lips as he lowered his head with painful slowness. His tongue-tip teased first one rosy peak of her breast and then the other. She gasped his name, her fingers threading through his dark hair, holding his head against her body, not wanting the tide of feelings he was arousing within her ever to stop.

His burning mouth sought the valley between her breasts and rose to press against the pulse that beat erratically at the base of her throat. Carolyn's fingers fumbled with the buttons of his shirt, pulling it open, running her hands over his hard flat midriff, over his taut masculine breast, through the mat of soft curling dark hair on his chest before swaying forward until her throbbing breasts touched his own naked chest.

A tiny purr of sensual pleasure escaped from deep

within her and Leith found her lips again, his kiss searing her, branding her for ever, lifting her senses impossibly higher.

'God, Carolyn, I want to make love to you,' he murmured huskily when breathlessly his mouth surrendered hers. 'I want you, more than I've ever wanted any other woman.' His hands propelled her hips against him, against the surge of his taut thighs, his straining arousal. 'Feel what you do to me?' he asked thickly, his blue eyes enmeshing her, enveloping her, until she knew she was drowning in their inky passion-filled depths.

When the phone rang Carolyn thought the shock of the jarring sound had stopped her heart beating. The intrusion held them immobile, poised together, very nearly at a peak that a split second later would have had them tumbling over and downwards into a sensual fulfilment she had craved as much as Leith had. But the ringing noise was enough to still her mindless burning and she tensed, suddenly realising how close she had come to completely surrendering herself, her body, to Leith McCabe.

Oh, no! No! How could she have? Panic rose inside her and she pushed her hands against his chest, striving to put some space between their heated bodies. For agonised seconds Leith held her fast and then he allowed her to stumble backwards, her face flushing fiery red as his eyes burned over her naked breasts, her taut nipples verifying the fact that she was still as phyically aroused as he made no attempt to disguise he was.

In one lithe movement he reached across and picked up the phone. 'McCabe,' his voice barked shortly. 'New York? All right, put it through.' His eyes watched Carolyn as she drew her robe about her, her fingers shaking uncontrollably. 'Quinlan? What's the trouble?' He listened impassively. 'Can't it wait until I fly over next month?'

He rubbed an irritated hand along his jaw line. 'Okay, I'll send Dave over as soon as I can contact him. Keep them hanging until then.' He replaced the receiver with controlled violence, his eyes darkening as he looked up to find Carolyn now had the width of the desk between them.

His lips twisted upwards in a derisive smile. 'That was the finest display of bad timing I've ever known,' he said, his eyes meeting hers.

Carolyn's gaze fell. 'Yes. I . . . I'll go to bed.' Her voice caught painfully in her throat.

'To bed,' he repeated flatly.

'Yes. I . . . I'm tired.'

'To bed alone, I take it?'

'Yes.' She drew a ragged breath. 'I think that would be best.'

'Do you, Carolyn?' His voice fell, sending tantalising shivers down Carolyn's spine, reawakening her still-smouldering arousal.

'Yes. I'm sorry if I gave you the wrong idea just now. I——'

His eyebrows rose. 'How could I have got the wrong idea?' he asked sarcastically. 'Surely not the fact that you were in my arms, all but in my bed, surely that wouldn't have given me the wrong idea?' His lips thinned angrily. 'And I could have had you there, in my bed, couldn't I, Carolyn? So very easily.'

His blue eyes impaled her and she was unable to look away. And the lie, the contradiction that rose inside her, she found impossible to voice.

'I guess I can't deny that.' She ran a shaky hand over her eyes. 'You seem to be able to . . . I do . . . find you attractive.' Her throat ached as she forced the words out. 'But I couldn't have faced myself in the morning. I don't sleep around, Leith. If that makes me old-fashioned, or some sort of oddity, then I'm sorry. But . . . I can't.'

Anger still held him tensely still and when he moved to stride around the desk she shook her head, holding out her hand to ward him off. Reaching her, he pulled her roughly into his arms, his lips swooping to claim hers punishingly until she whimpered in protest. Yet even as she did so, as her hands strove to push him away from her, part of her was responding to his nearness, his bruising kiss.

And he sensed that response, raising his head to gaze down at her in triumph, his breathing raw and ragged. Pain tore at her and she knew it was reflected in her eyes as she looked up at him pleadingly.

'Please, Leith, don't do this.'

He held her in his vicelike grip for immeasurable moments while she watched the warring of his emotions. Then he released her, thrust her from him, and he turned away from her.

Carolyn slowly expelled the breath she had been holding, knowing that some traitorous part of her wished desperately that he hadn't let her go. She knew she should make a break for her room, but something held her motionless. She took a few shaky steps towards him and her hand reached out to touch his arm. He flinched, moving out of her reach.

'Leith, I'm sorry,' she gulped, a heavy coldness clutching at her heart.

He remained where he was, his back stiff and uncompromising and he ran a hand tiredly through his hair. 'Go to bed, Carolyn,' he said flatly. 'And you'd better go now, while I'm still capable of letting you,' he added almost self-derisively.

Leith left early next morning for the construction site accompanied by Joe Dawson, leaving Carolyn to catch up on the office work. The short time they'd spent together had been an agony for her, but Leith was as cool and businesslike as he'd ever been—so much so that Carolyn could almost believe those torrid moments the night before had never happened. And Leith bore no signs of a sleepless night while she had had to use her make-up to disguise the dark smudges under her eyes that were a legacy of her tossing and turning in her suddenly very large, very lonely bed.

She tried to tell herself she had made the right decision, but it was cold comfort when her totally aroused senses craved the satisfaction she knew instinctively Leith's hard body could give her. The temptation to clamber out of bed and run in search of him had been almost overwhelming—but she made herself remember the inquest and the young Leith McCabe's cold unforgiving anger.

She had a solitary lunch in their suite and then began on the few letters Leith had left for her to type, only to be interrupted by a knock on the door. She crossed the room and put her eye to the peephole. Peter Kruger stood outside, and Carolyn hesitated before slowly opening the door.

'What do you want, Peter?' she asked evenly.

'If I said you, would you slam the door in my face?' he asked with his most charming smile.

Her lips tightened and he shrugged theatrically.

'Okay. Is McCabe here?'

'No, he isn't.' Carolyn kept him standing in the hallway.

'When will he be back?'

She glanced at her watch. 'Not for half an hour or so.'

Peter frowned. 'Look, Carolyn, I particularly wanted to see him, to apologise.'

She raised her eyebrows.

'I didn't exactly welcome him with open arms and maybe we got off on the wrong foot. I'd like to remedy that. Can I come in and wait for him?'

He seemed to be quite serious, and after a moment Carolyn stepped back and held the door open. 'Well, all right. But I can't promise he'll be back in half an hour. You may have a long wait.'

'That's okay.' He walked past her and into the room.

Carolyn slowly closed the door and followed him, reseating herself at her typewriter as Peter prowled around.

'Mind if I pour myself a drink?'

'No.' She began typing.

'Do you want one?'

She shook her head and finished her letter, pulling it out of the machine and setting it on the pile awaiting Leith's signature.

'I meant to ask you how Dad's farewell went.' He paused in front of her desk.

'It went well. Everyone was there,' she said smoothly.

'Yes, I was sorry I couldn't make it, but,' he shrugged, 'you know how it is.' He swallowed his drink in one gulp and gazed down at the empty glass. 'I suppose I'm something of a disappointment to my father. I know he expected more of me, for me to take over Kruger's, but I'm not in McCabe's league, am I?'

Carolyn stood up and covered her typewriter, more than a little surprised by Peter's change of attitude.

'Few men are, wouldn't you say, Carolyn?'

'I suppose not,' she replied evenly. 'He does work hard.'

He moved around to sit on the edge of her desk. 'Has he said anything about how he plans to get the complex back on schedule?' he asked with studied casualness.

'No.'

'No, you don't know or no, you're not telling?' he probed.

'No, I don't know, Peter,' she said distinctly.

'What about the contractors? Is he going to change those?' he persisted.

'I have no idea. You'll have to ask him.' Carolyn slid everything into her drawer and turned the key. She glanced across at him and the easy charm left his face as he stood up angrily.

'Fat chance he'll tell me,' he muttered and took a couple of steps that brought him up to her. 'Come on, Carolyn. What would it hurt to tell me? If not for me then for my father.'

Carolyn's first instinctive reaction to his nearness was

to step away from him, but she held her ground. 'What's your father got to do with it?'

'Well, I was under the impression you thought a lot of the old man and he's going to be pretty upset if all this reflects badly on me.'

She gasped in amazement that quickly changed to angry dislike. She shook her head and went to turn away from him, but his hand closed on her arm, bruising her, jerking her back to face him.

'There you go again, sweet Carolyn,' he sneered. 'Don't turn your back on me. How do you think the great Leith McCabe will react when I tell him his precious secretary gave me important information from his confidential file,' he paused triumphantly, 'in return for certain personal, more intimate favours?'

Her stomach twisted nauseously. 'I think you'd better leave, Peter. That's an empty threat and you know it.'

'Is it? I saw enough in the files the other day to make it convincing,' he smiled maliciously.

'What possible reason could you have for telling Leith such lies?' she asked him quietly, scarcely believing this could be happening.

'Call it an appropriate revenge if you like, for all the put-downs you've given me.'

'What would you gain by it?' She shook her head. 'It wouldn't be worth it, Peter.'

'No? I think it would. I have this gut feeling Mr NatCon himself wouldn't care to know he was having my cast-off.'

Carolyn stared at him uncomprehendingly. 'Cast-off?'

'Don't play dumb, Carolyn. Cast-off. One I've used and discarded. You.'

She strained from him in revulsion, but he held her fast.

'However, for just a little more inside information, dear Carolyn, I might be encouraged to abandon my vengeful ways.'

Her lips curled. 'If you think for one moment I'd let

you blackmail me into . . . You must be mad!' She didn't even attempt to keep the contempt out of her voice and the anger that blazed in his eyes had her fighting to free his grip on her arm.

'I swear I'll break you, you cold little bitch!' He dragged her against him, and as his lips swooped downwards she turned her mouth away, straining against the hold of his restricting hands, and she heard the bodice of her dress tear as his lips captured hers almost ferociously.

She felt the bile rise in her throat and her teeth clamped down on his lip. She felt no compunction as she bit him hard. He staggered backwards, his hand going to his mouth and coming away with a smear of blood. He used an obscenity Carolyn had never before actually heard anyone say and made to come after her. But just as suddenly he was stopped in his tracks as Leith hauled him backwards.

'That's enough, Kruger,' he commanded evenly.

Peter almost overbalanced as Leith released him and he was breathing heavily, his eyes flashing pure venom as he looked from Leith back to Carolyn.

'Get out,' ordered Leith with deceptive quietness. 'And don't bother coming back, Kruger. You're through!'

Peter pulled himself upright. 'Am I, McCabe?' His eyes raked Carolyn and his fingers gingerly touched his swelling lip. 'Maybe you should ask Carolyn how I come to know about the change of contractors and your plans to swap distributors!'

Carolyn started forward, but Leith halted her with a movement of his hand. 'The way things are anyone with half a brain could have guessed at those changes, Kruger, and I'd say you would be the last person to draw attention to the dealings with the contractors. Do you need help to the door?'

Peter's face paled slightly but he defiantly stood his

ground. 'I'll get you for this, McCabe! When my father hears——'

Leith cut him off. 'I've already spoken to your father. Now, get out.'

Peter hesitated, his hands bunched into fists, but whatever he read in Leith's face made him turn, swearing, leaving the suite and slamming the door after him.

Carolyn's body sagged and she clutched at her torn dress. 'Leith, I didn't tell him anything. I caught him looking at the file on Monday when I——'

Leith reached out and gently drew her into his arms. 'I know,' he said softly, his hand tenderly moving against her back. 'I heard enough of it to fill in the rest.'

She sighed brokenly. 'I didn't want you to think that I'd . . .' She shuddered.

Leith's fingers lifted her chin and he kissed her lightly on her nose. 'I don't.'

She gazed up at him and the burning desire only he could start rose inside her, glowed in her smoky grey eyes. Leith's muscles tensed and then he had put her away from him.

'Go put on your swimsuit. We're taking the afternoon off,' he said firmly.

'But——'

'No buts, Carolyn.' He turned her in the direction of her room and gave her a little push. 'I'd say we deserve to play truant!'

The turquoise water broke mildly on the clean sand and green palms waved around the small secluded little beach.

'How did you find this?' asked Carolyn as she wriggled her bare toes in the warm sand.

Leith was beginning to unbutton his shirt and he smiled easily. 'Kim and his wife were telling me about it last night. It sounded just what we needed.'

She stood watching him and his smile was just as

dazzling as the sunlight shining on the sand and sea, and the effect it had on Carolyn was almost as stunning. He pulled his shirt out of the waistband of his slacks and shrugged it off. When he reached for his belt, undoing the buckle, she turned slightly away, shakily slipping her loose blouse over her head and then stepping out of her skirt.

Her blue bikini was modest by modern standards but as Leith's eyes ran over her Carolyn's skin burned, leaving her feeling gloriously naked and alive with the desire to feel his hands on her body. And her own eyes drank in the hard perfection of his lithe, lightly tanned body. He wore brief black trunks, and when she dragged her gaze upwards to meet his she could see that answering liquid fire flaring in their blue depths.

'Let's swim,' he said huskily, and held out his hand. Without reservation Carolyn slipped her hand into his and they ran down to the water together.

The first mild chill was invigorating and they swam together stroke for stroke into the deeper water. Eventually she stopped and trod water watching Leith power through the sea with easy proficient strokes. Rolling on her back she let herself float, her eyes gazing up in wonder at the pure blue of the cloudless sky. It was so peaceful she wished she could hang in the warm water and never have to think about anything.

About Peter Kruger's terrible display. About telling Bodie the whole truth about his father. About this growing attraction between herself and Leith McCabe and what she was going to do about it, what she knew she should be doing about it. She closed her eyes tightly. How she wished she didn't have to back away, keep him out of her life.

The surface broke, jostling her floating body, and she opened her eyes as Leith flicked the water from his dark hair.

'How about a race back to the beach? Do you need a start?' he teased, and Carolyn took up his challenge.

Only in the last few metres did he forge slightly ahead, and he turned to face her as their feet found the soft sandy bottom.

'No wonder Bodie swims so well,' he said as they waded into the shallows. 'His mother is definitely no slouch in the water herself.'

Carolyn smiled and brushed her wet unconfined hair back from her face. As she did so she stood on something sharp and couldn't hold back a gasp of pain.

Leith turned as she hopped on one foot, the water still lapping her knees. 'What is it?' he asked as she lifted her foot to see if the skin had been broken.

'I stood on something,' she told him, gingerly feeling the sole of her foot, 'but it's not bleeding. Must have been a stone or a shell.'

Leith bent over to have a look, his fingers gentle on her skin as she put her hand on his shoulder to balance herself.

'How does it feel now?' He pressed her foot.

'Okay. Just a bit bruised, I think.'

'Can you walk on it?'

Carolyn tested it carefully. 'Mmm, it seems all right.'

Before she realised what he was about Leith had lifted her into his arms, carrying her up the sand to where they had left their towels. Carolyn's arms slid around him and the gentle abrasion of their damp salty skin took her mind well away from her sore foot. He stopped and slowly set her down, his eyes locked with hers, his hands lingering on her waist, slowly drawing her closer against his hard body.

And then they were clinging together, their passion flaring, raging, bursting about them in a searing flame of desire. Their bodies were moulded, fused together. Leith kissed her eyes, her nose, her lips, hot scorching kisses. He nibbled her earlobe, burned a trail of fire down to the pulse at the base of her throat, downwards to seek and discover the valley between her breasts cupped in her bikini top. They sank down on to the sand, their legs entwined, and Leith unclipped her bra top, gazing down at her full naked breasts for long earth-shattering moments before his hand slid up over her flat stomach to cup one pearly mound.

With tortuous slowness his fingertip encircled one taut thrusting point and then the other. Carolyn moaned softly, arching to meet his seeking mouth as his tongue-tip traced the path of his fingertip.

Her own hands clutched at his back, sliding over the firm masculine contours, down over his lean hips, her fingers trembling as they ran lightly along his thigh. She felt his response as he moved against her and she completely lost her head. She strained towards him until they were thigh to thigh, stomach to stomach, breast to breast, and he claimed her lips with a kiss that reached down into her very soul. When his mouth surrendered hers they were both breathless.

'God, Carolyn, you feel so good! I've wanted you back in my arms ever since last night—desperately so.' He gazed down into her eyes, his own brilliant with barely contained passion. 'You'll never know how hard it was for me to let you go,' he said thickly. 'I ended up going down to the pool and I lost count of the number of lengths I swam. If I'd stayed in the suite with you so close I . . .'

He drew her to him fiercely, his head between her breasts, his lips hot on her tingling skin. His hands cupped her buttocks, fingers sliding beneath the material of her bikini bottom, to guide her closer to his male hardness.

'Leith, I——' Carolyn swallowed as a wave of all-consuming desire rose to engulf her. She needed to tell him how much she loved him, wanted him, ached for him to make love to her. Here. Now. But his hands released her, rose to frame her face and he looked down at her tenderly.

'I know—you're not that kind of girl,' he quipped with a crooked smile, wiping a wet strand of hair back behind her ear. 'And I respect that. I'm not going to pressure you, even if I do just go quietly insane,' he added brokenly, his eyes drinking in the still-taut invitation of her breasts.

His eyes rose to meet hers and his face was all seriousness. 'Marry me, Carolyn?' he asked softly, his burning gaze holding her immobile. 'I can't live without you.'

CHAPTER EIGHT

'COLD, Mum?' asked Bodie as the tram carried them back to the hostel where they were staying.

'It is a little chilly, but we're nearly there,' Carolyn said as evenly as she could. It wasn't the temperature that had made her shiver; it was the thought of seeing Leith again. They had parted at Brisbane airport last Friday and he had continued on down to Tasmania to brief his brother on some trouble they were having in the States.

On Saturday Carolyn and Bodie had flown to Melbourne with Queensland's team for the Pacific School Games, and they had booked into a hostel that was within easy reach of the State Swimming Centre in Batman Avenue. The hostel was shabby but clean and didn't put too much strain on them financially.

Now it was Monday and Leith had left a message at the hostel that he would be calling to see them at six o'clock. Carolyn shivered again. She found it an impossibility to wipe from her mind the ecstasy of the feel of his hands moving over her body, his deep drugging kisses. And her body craved him now, after only three days' separation.

'It's great Mr McCabe's calling tonight, isn't it, Mum?' Bodie's voice broke in on her sybaritic thoughts. 'I wonder what sort of car he drives down here in Melbourne.'

'I don't know,' Carolyn murmured absently. Had she really agreed to marry him? Her mouth went dry and her heartbeats fluttered erratically. How could she have accepted his proposal? If he found out about——? He never will, she told herself for the hundredth time. How could he? It was all a long time ago, a nine-days' wonder at that, and people forgot.

While they were together in Fiji it had all seemed so simple. She only had to look at him and her sudden doubts flew out of the window. But she had had three days without him to think about it and her heart contracted in fear, alternating betwen a desire to tell him the truth now before he found out, and an hysterical urge to hide it from him at all costs, grabbing at happiness while she could. Either way she was caught on a very slippery tightrope, one she had stepped on to and now couldn't get off.

She had made several attempts to tell Bodie about her marriage to Leith, but each time the words wouldn't come. Knowing how delighted he would be she hadn't wanted to build him up only to have him disappointed when she told Leith she had changed her mind. Changed her mind? She could almost laugh out loud at that. She would never change her mind about the depth of her love for Leith McCabe.

Now everything was snowballing, drawing her into a web of self-destruction. And she was enmeshed.

'I'm dying to show Mr McCabe my medals,' Bodie was saying.

Carolyn drew herself together and smiled at him. 'One bronze yesterday and two gold and a silver today—four medals out of four events isn't bad,' she agreed. 'You have every right to be pleased with yourself.'

'I'm just glad I didn't let Coach down, or the team.' He sighed. 'You don't suppose Mr McCabe will come with us tonight, do you?'

'We haven't got a ticket for him, love,' Carolyn began, and Bodie sheepishly dug into the pocket of his tracksuit.

'I heard Mr Carson saying someone couldn't come tonight, so I asked him for the ticket. I said it was for a really great friend.' He showed his mother the ticket. 'Got a cheek, haven't I?'

'Oh, Bodie, you shouldn't have done that!'

'Maybe not, but nobody's using it and if he's free—Mr McCabe, I mean—well, he can come, too.'

Carolyn frowned slightly. 'Don't get your heart set on it, Bodie. He may be busy.'

'I know. But it won't hurt to ask him. Here's our stop.' Bodie stood up.

Carolyn's nervous fingers shook so badly she couldn't get her hair to stay in its chignon. Taking a deep breath, she let it fall to her shoulders and ran a tidying brush through it.

She gazed at her reflection in the shabby mirror, at the glow in her eyes, the soft inviting curve of her lips. Could just the thought of Leith McCabe do this to her, bring her features to life, set every nerve-ending in her body tingling with anticipation?

The evening they had spent alone together before they left Fiji came vividly back to her and a warm flush rose to colour her cheeks. After finishing the office work they had swum in the pool and finished off with a revitalising shower before walking arm in arm back to the suite. Once inside Leith had turned her into his arms, kissing her deeply, lingeringly. She had drowned in that kiss, in his continued so-arousing caresses.

'I've been wanting to do that for hours,' he had said brokenly. 'You feel so good!'

Both their robes had fallen discarded to the floor and their agitated fingers had explored each other. Carolyn had pressed closer to him, running her lips along the smooth warmth of his shoulder as her hands played over his lean hips, the indentation of his backbone, and he had groaned huskily.

With fingers that shook slightly he had unclasped her

bikini top and his hands had slid around to cup her breasts, to tease the incited hardness of her nipples and she strained against him. The response of his arousal had caught her breath in her throat and she could only gaze up at him, her eyes large and luminous, and unconsciously alluring.

He had drawn her to him and the sensitised hardness of her breasts had rasped deliriously against his bare chest, filling her with an urgent, thought-destroying desire to feel the whole long naked length of him beside her. She had murmured his name brokenly, her fingers moving to the elasticised band of his brief swim-shorts. His hand had covered hers, staying it.

'Carolyn, we'd better cool down or I won't be able to hold back,' he had said huskily.

'I don't want you to,' she had whispered, raining soft kisses on his chin.

'Caro, please! I want it to be right for you, our wedding, our wedding night.' He had threaded his fingers through her hair. 'Darling, I can wait.'

'Oh, Leith, it is right.' She had let her fingertips trail tantalisingly downwards over his body. 'I want you so much. Right now. Don't you want me?'

He had crushed her to him. 'Caro, you're sure?' he had asked unsteadily, and she had nodded and kissed him.

For a split second he had remained still, poised, his eyes brilliant blue, full of an electrifying promise as he gazed down at her. Then with arms around each other they had walked through to his bedroom. He had quickly dispensed with her bikini bottom and then his own trunks. Laying her on the bed, his naked body had followed hers, stretching out beside her, burning where their heated skin touched.

Carolyn had moaned softly in her throat, a sound she scarcely recognised as her own voice, as Leith had kissed her mouth, the hollow of her neck, her breasts, his hands caressing each secret place until she ached for fulfilment.

He had moved his body over hers, parting her legs with

his own, and she knew a moment of panic. Leith had stilled, taking his weight on one arm, his other hand gently stroking her cheek.

'Carolyn, I love you,' he said thickly. 'Don't stop me now.'

'No. I . . . It's just that I . . .' Carolyn had swallowed, her hands running agitatedly over the tensed muscles of his back. 'There's been no one since Bodie's father and I . . .'

'Oh, Caro, Caro,' he had murmured, his lips tenderly nibbling hers. 'We'll go slowly.'

And when he had finally entered her Carolyn arched to meet him, a wave of desire rippling over her, a surge that grew into a flood, a deluge that swept them along together until they cried out in unison as they soared on the crest of pure rapturous abandonment.

Breathlessly they had both floated back to earth and Leith had lifted himself from her to lie beside her, holding her in the circle of his arms.

'God, Caro, that was beautiful,' he had breathed huskily. 'I didn't hurt you, did I?'

She had shaken her head, burrowing a kiss into the curve of his throat. 'You were wonderful,' she had sighed, smiling up at him. 'Just wonderful!'

Leith had chuckled, a vibrantly masculine sound that thrilled her, rekindling her desire, and she had run tantalising fingers sensuously over his body. He had groaned deep in his throat.

'Good grief, the lady's insatiable!' he had laughed softly, his lips claiming hers as she felt the throb of his response beneath her caressing fingers.

Passion had risen to wrap them in its time-stopping cocoon as they moved together, as one, until they had tumbled to a climax that left them drowsily euphoric. Carolyn had sighed, expelling a deep soft murmur as she stretched her enervated muscles.

'Mmm,' she murmured drowsily.

'Just mmm?' Leith had rested on his elbow and looked down at her.

'Well, how about, now I know?' She had run her finger along the line of his jaw.

He had raised his eyebrow enquiringly and she chuckled.

'That you're not just a pretty face,' she had elaborated, her eyes dancing.

'You mean I have your stamp of approval?' he had asked with mock incredulity.

Carolyn's fingers had cupped his face. 'This stamp of approval, and this one, and this one,' she had said, interspersing her words with quick light kisses, and he laughed.

'You know, I could quite cheerfully have throttled that damned messenger boy in the lift. He completely wrecked my plan.'

'What plan?'

'To get you into my arms by fair means or foul. Once I had you there I knew I could persuade you to see things my way,' he had explained confidently, and Carolyn had tried unsuccessfully to push him away from her.

'Of all the arrogant, chauvinistic . . .'

Her words had been lost in his mouth as he covered her lips with his own. Carolyn's hands had given up the fight, sliding around him as she responded to his kiss without a shred of reservation.

When Leith had raised his head he had drawn a shaky breath before smiling down at her. 'Perhaps it's as well I didn't kiss you in the lift. We might have given the messenger boy the shock of his young life. But my plan did work, didn't it?' he had asked, softly teasing.

'It has the makings of a successful scheme but,' she had tried to keep a straight face, 'I suggest you keep working on it. Who knows to what heights it might rise?'

They had both laughed together and Leith had drawn her tenderly into his arms, cradling her head on his shoulder, and they had fallen asleep in each other's arms.

Now, in her room in the shabby hostel, Carolyn yearned desperately to be back in those strong arms, safe, unthinking——

The knock on her door brought her mind back to the present as she started, the sound nearly frightening her to death. She glanced at her watch. Five-thirty. Perhaps Bodie had forgotten something. Crossing the room, she opened the door.

In the dingy hallway he looked bigger, darker, far more potently attractive, and her heart leapt, flipping over as their eyes met. Leith stepped into the room, threw his jacket on to the bed and wrapped her in his arms.

'God, I've missed you,' he groaned huskily, and then their lips met, quick scorching caresses that developed into longer, deeper, blazing kisses. And Carolyn clung to him. She could no more have pulled away from him than she could have flown.

Leith reluctantly raised his head. 'Carolyn Allerton, you're in my blood and I have a feeling if I can't get to hold you, kiss you, at least once a day I'm going to be totally useless to everyone.' He looked down at her tenderly. 'Dave, my brother, asked me if I was sickening for something.'

'And what did you say?' Carolyn put her finger to his lips and he nibbled it gently.

'I just smiled and told him to be prepared for a surprise in the very near future. He flew off to the States with a puzzled look on his face that means my sister will be around to check up on me as soon as Dave can contact her,' he laughed. 'Where's Bodie? Have you told him? How did he take it?'

'He's . . . he's down at the bathroom having a shower, and I haven't exactly—well,' Leith was watching her levelly, 'I didn't want to get him excited before the Games, so I haven't told him yet.' And besides, Carolyn thought shakily, I couldn't believe it myself.

'He should know, Carolyn,' Leith said firmly, 'so that he can get used to the idea. I want us to be married as soon as possible.' His eyes fell to the curve of her lips. 'I want my ring on your finger.' His voice was huskily unsteady and his mouth claimed hers almost desperately.

A discreet cough penetrated Carolyn's euphoric aura and she pulled back in the circle of Leith's arms to see Bodie standing in the open doorway, his towel slung over his shoulder, a broad grin on his face. Leith turned his head and he smiled easily at Bodie.

'I suppose you want to know my intentions?' he said amusedly. 'Rest assured they're most definitely honourable! I intend to marry your mother as soon as we can deal with all the red tape. With your blessing, of course.' He stood away from Carolyn but held her hand firmly in his, and his face was serious now. 'What do you think, Bodie?'

'What do I think?' Bodie's smile widened. 'I think it's great! Fantastic!' He took two strides across the room and gave his mother a hug. Then he turned to Leith, went to hug him, too, and with an uncharacteristic blush, held out his hand.

Leith took it and then wrapped his arms around the boy, giving him a quick squeeze, his eyes meeting Carolyn's over Bodie's head.

'This is just great!' Bodie repeated, almost jumping up and down with pleasure, and Carolyn pulled her eyes from Leith to turn to her son.

'Don't go getting too excited, love,' she warned. 'You have to swim tonight.'

Bodie laughed. 'I'm staying very cool about the swimming, but I'm getting pretty excited about you two getting married. Wait till I tell Brett!'

'I'm glad you're pleased, Bodie,' Leith said quietly. 'That means a lot to me, and to your mother.'

Bodie sobered. 'I guess you know my dad died before I was born, so I've never had a father, Mr McCabe.'

'Leith,' he put in.

'Leith,' Bodie repeated. 'And—well, I want you to know I don't think Mum could have chosen anyone I'd like more,' he stopped and swallowed, and Carolyn put her arms around him, her eyes full of tears.

After a moment Bodie laughed huskily. 'What a day. I get three medals this afternoon and a father this evening. Unreal!' He turned to his mother. 'Did you, you know, ask about tonight?'

Carolyn looked at Leith. 'What Bodie means is we have a spare ticket for the swimming tonight and we wondered if you could come.'

'I wouldn't miss it,' he said, and Bodie's face glowed.

'I just had a feeling about tonight,' said Bodie from the back seat as Leith drove them home later that night. 'I couldn't believe it when I got the second fastest time in the heats, but in the final, standing on the blocks, I really knew I was going to win the gold.'

Leith pulled up outside the ill-lit hostel and as they climbed from the car a weaving untidy figure lurched drunkenly past them. Leith's gaze followed the man's retreating form and then turned to the ancient façade of the building and he paused.

'How long will it take you to pack?' he asked, and Carolyn stared at him.

'Pack? What for?'

'This is no place for you and Bodie. I have a perfectly comfortable apartment and it's much closer to the swimming venue.'

'But——' Carolyn began.

'I insist, Carolyn,' he said firmly. 'Let's get your things. Come on, Bodie.'

Leith's apartment was on the top floor of the building and the view from the living-room window was nothing short of spectacular. The whole place was straight out of a glossy magazine, Carolyn decided, as she stood gazing about her, sure she had to be dreaming. None of this could be real. Leith loving her. His proposal. The apartment.

The living-room was decorated in creams and blues

and although it was quietly opulent it had a lived-in atmosphere, books on the coffee-table and photographs, family shots Carolyn couldn't bear to let herself look at, on the sideboard.

Bodie sat experimentally in a large lounge chair. 'Wow! This is really something.'

Leith's lips twitched. 'Bring your gear, Bodie, and I'll show you your room.'

Carolyn followed them, her eyes drinking in the subtle decor. It wasn't at all what she expected. This was no suave bachelor pad; it was a comfortable, if luxurious, home.

Leith left Bodie to settle into his room and opened a door further along the hallway.

'Leith——' Carolyn paused. 'With Bodie here—well, I can't——' Her voice faded away.

'I know, love, and I understand,' he said softly as he set down her case. 'I'm across the hall.' His lips twisted ruefully. 'I must be mad. I'll need a dozen cold showers thinking about you in here, so close, so beautiful.'

He pulled her into his arms and kissed her lingeringly. Carolyn melted against him and his hands moved sensually over her back. A surge of wanting rose within her and her heart swelled with love for him until the ache for him was a physical pain. And just as suddenly, as acutely, a wave of pure foreboding gripped her. Fear clutched at her telling her to enjoy her happiness while she could for as long as it lasted. Her arms around his neck tightened convulsively and Leith looked down at her.

'What's the matter?'

Carolyn closed her eyes tightly and opened them again to gaze up at him. 'I'm just frightened.'

'Frightened? Of what?' he smiled tenderly.

'Because I'm so happy.' Tell him now, she commanded herself, tell him now, before it's too late.

His fingers gently trailed over her cheek, traced the

line of her jaw. 'What's so frightening about being happy?'

'Oh, Leith, I——' she gulped. 'There are things about me you . . . you don't know. I mean, we've known each other for such a short time, only weeks, and——'

'And I love you,' he finished quietly.

Her heart turned over. 'I love you, too,' she said intensely, 'so very much. That's why I have to tell you——'

'Carolyn, I already know your dreadful secret,' he said lightly, and Carolyn's head snapped up to meet his amused gaze.

'You know?' The words were barely a whisper.

'I can hazard a guess. I'd say you weren't married when you had Bodie. Am I right?'

Carolyn was so stunned she couldn't find her voice. She nodded slowly and Leith drew her against him, cradling her head against his shoulder.

'Do you think that could possibly make any difference to the way I feel about you? he asked thickly. 'You were only a kid.'

She felt a tight knot of tears burn behind her eyes as guilt clutched her. Tell him all of it. 'Oh, Leith, hold me,' she whispered desperately, and his arms tightened around her before his lips found hers again as she clung to him. When he surrendered her lips he smiled crookedly down at her.

'I rest my case,' he said evenly. He kissed the tip of her nose, reluctantly putting her from him. 'And I think we need a cup of coffee before I see you to your lonely bed and try to keep my mind off that night in Fiji!'

The next day was Bodie's final day of competition and Leith accompanied them to the swimming centre. Bodie put on a sparkling performance, collecting two more gold medals, bringing his tally for the games to five gold, one silver and one bronze. His coach was ecstatic, but Bodie seemed happier about having Leith there as his prospective stepfather.

That evening Leith took them out to dinner, and as he had to go into the office on Wednesday Carolyn and Bodie went along to the final day's swimming as spectators. On Thursday, the day before they were due to fly back to Brisbane, Bodie accompanied his team-mates on a planned excursion and Leith took Carolyn to an élite jewellers to choose her engagement ring.

They lunched at a small secluded restaurant, and although Carolyn couldn't have said later what they discussed, they seemed to talk for hours. And they held hands, smiling at each other.

Back at the apartment she gazed down at the sparkling beauty of the diamond and emerald ring on her left hand, hardly daring to believe it was there. She looked up to find Leith watching her and she gave a shaky laugh.

'It's so beautiful!'

He pulled her easily into his arms. 'Not as beautiful as you are,' he said softly, kissing her with slow sensuousness.

Somehow they were on the couch, his hands caressing her, his lips tantalising, drugging, then starting a fire inside her that quickly raged out of control. Her trembling fingers found the buttons on his shirt, parting the silky material, and she slid her hands inside over his smooth satin flesh.

Leith's own hands slipped beneath her thin-knit blouse to cup her breasts, teasing her throbbing nipples through the fine lace of her bra. The fire in Carolyn seared at his touch and she bent her head, running her lips over the flat hardness of his midriff. Her tongue-tip circled his male nipple and he groaned throatily.

Beneath her she was aware of the strength of his arousal as he deftly removed her blouse and unhooked her bra so that he could gaze down at her full naked breasts. His lips trailed fire downwards, his mouth climbing and conquering first one burning peak and then the other. Carolyn's fingers twisted deliriously in his thick dark hair, holding his head against her body.

'Oh, Leith, love me,' she murmured thickly, scarcely aware she'd spoken the words aloud.

'Do you know I've been thinking of you like this ever since Fiji? It seems like an eternity ago.' He lifted her effortlessly and carried her along the hall to his room. 'Did I dream it all, Caro?' he asked as he lay down beside her, folding her passionately into his arms, so close she could feel the heavy thudding of his heart beneath her hand.

'Not one beautiful moment of it,' she told him, her voice husky with a burning desire, her lips moving along the strong column of his throat.

Leith's fingers played over her heated skin, finding each sensitive spot, making her catch her breath and arch her body towards his, moving with him until they were lost in each other, surging upwards on a wave of pure ecstasy.

Later Carolyn gave a soft satisfied laugh. 'Do I look like a cat who's just stolen the cream?'

Leith was looking down at her and his mouth turned upwards in a smile that drove deep creases in his cheeks. 'You have the look, my love, of a very contented pussycat.'

Carolyn expelled a soft throaty purring sound. 'A very contented pussycat,' she agreed, running her hand lightly over his broad shoulder.

He sobered, his eyes holding hers. 'You're not sorry we haven't waited until we're married?'

She sat up, pushing him back on to the bed, resting her hands on his chest, her chin on her hands. 'Not one tiny little bit,' she told him honestly, raising herself a little until their lips met.

Leith folded his arms around her, rolling her over, reversing their positions. 'Mm, Caro. How have I existed without you?'

Without you. The words echoed inside her and she shivered. Without him. No, not now. She couldn't bear to lose him. She'd never tell him. Never let him find out.

'Are you cold?' he asked solicitously, and she shook her head.

'No. But I think I should get dressed. Bodie will be back soon and I want to get myself together before he comes. I have a feeling at the moment I look a little like a woman who's been made love to most satisfactorily, hmm?'

'Very much so,' Leith laughed. 'And Bodie's going to have to get used to that look,' he added with masculine arrogance.

Bodie was regaling them with the details of his excursion later that evening when the doorbell pealed. Leith crossed to open the door and a fair haired girl threw herself into his arms.

'Leith! We were hoping you'd be home.' She kissed him enthusiastically on the cheek and turned to the tall man behind her. 'I told you he would be, darling.' At that moment she caught sight of Carolyn and Bodie and she paused in surprise. 'Oh dear, I hope we're not interrupting.'

'Something tells me that fact wouldn't bother your pretty head for a moment,' Leith said drily. 'Come on in. How are you, Tim?' he directed at the man.

'Fine, Leith,' he gave an apologetic grin. 'We had a call from Dave yesterday.'

Leith raised a sardonic eyebrow. 'I thought you might have.'

Carolyn had struggled slowly to her feet, her eyes taking in the other girl's features. She was fair-haired and very attractive and Carolyn knew she was about her own age. In the fourteen years she hadn't changed all that much. There was still that striking resemblance to her brother—her younger brother. Carolyn's heart pounded inside her breast as she waited tensely for Leith's sister to recognise her.

'Carolyn,' Leith was beside her, sliding his arm around her waist, his firm hand pulling her against him. 'This is my sister, Suzy, and her husband, Tim Blair. Meet

Carolyn Allerton and her son, Bodie. Carolyn and I are getting married.'

'Oh, Leith, that's wonderful.' Suzy flung her arms around her brother again. 'So Dave was right.' She turned to Carolyn and hugged her, too. 'You don't know how happy we are that Leith's finally taking the plunge. We thought he was going to be the proverbial crusty old bachelor uncle!' She greeted Bodie as her husband quietly shook hands with Carolyn.

'Have you told Mum and Dad yet?' Suzy asked as Carolyn shakily expelled the breath she'd been holding.

Leith grimaced. 'I had hoped to keep our marriage to ourselves for a little longer,' he said meaningfully, 'before casting her into the midst of our overwhelming family. However, I suppose Dave will have spoken to Mum and Dad by now, so I'll ring them tomorrow.' He gave Carolyn a squeeze. 'Our parents are touring the States for a couple of months' holiday,' he explained.

Carolyn's tortured mind flashed a picture of Leith's mother in the hall of the Court House, a short woman dabbing her reddened eyes with her handkerchief. And Leith's father, as tall as his son, pulling Leith away from the frightened sixteen-year-old she had been then. Her stomach turned over in the painful grip of remembered guilt and fear.

'When's the wedding?' Suzy was asking her.

'Well, we haven't——' she began.

'Next month,' Leith replied. 'In Brisbane, and a small family affair. Definitely no publicity.'

Suzy made a disappointed moue at her brother. 'Spoilsport! And is your family in Brisbane, Carolyn?' she asked.

'No,' Carolyn replied uneasily. The web was tightening again, drawing her fatally into a situation she was convinced she should flee but knew just as surely she wouldn't even try to escape. 'My parents were divorced when I was a child. We've drifted apart and don't see each other at all. There's just Bodie and myself,' she added as evenly as she could.

'I must say you've kept all this very hush-hush. You didn't even hint that you were thinking of marriage when I saw you in Brisbane a few weeks ago.' Suzy grinned as Leith handed her a drink.

'At that time Carolyn wasn't giving me very encouraging vibes,' he said easily.

'I don't believe it,' Suzy laughed. 'That I would dearly love to have seen!'

Suzy. The scene in Leith's office fell into place. The mysterious woman on the phone had been his sister. Carolyn could almost laugh at herself.

'Mum and Dad will be over the moon when they hear Leith's getting married.' Suzy turned back to Carolyn. 'It's been a constant disappointment for them that both their sons have remained unmarried and haven't provided a continuation of the family name.'

Carolyn shot a startled glance at Leith and his eyes glowed, sending a silent message that brought their afternoon into vivid detail and she felt her cheeks grow warm. To have Leith's child—Her lashes fell in case he saw the pain and fear reflected there in her eyes. She just couldn't lose him now.

CHAPTER NINE

THE following weeks flew by as though they had wings. There seemed no time to think about anything and there were times in the office when Carolyn wondered if she had dreamed her engagement to Leith. Then she would touch the ring on her finger or she would catch the deep burning glow in Leith's gaze as their eyes met and her heart would turn over in her breast.

Maggie was promoted from the typing pool to take

over from Carolyn and they worked together while Maggie familiarised herself with the job. The whole building was agog with the news of the boss's engagement to his secretary.

Then the wedding was a mere week away. The staff gave Carolyn a small party as she was finishing work and it was during this get-together that Leith received a phone call from Joe Dawson in Fiji. It seemed Peter Kruger had been caught trying to sabotage some of the machinery and Leith flew out the next morning. Carolyn drove him to the airport.

'Suzy will ring you on Tuesday when she arrives in Brisbane,' he told her. 'If I'm not back she'll take you out to the airport to collect Mum and Dad on Thursday.'

Carolyn shivered, and when his flight was called she clung to him, suddenly afraid again.

'Damn Peter Kruger!' Leith swore huskily as his lips released her mouth, his eyes burning down into hers. 'I'll clear this trouble up as quickly as I can.'

Carolyn laughed shakily, swallowing a knot of tears. 'I hope you'll be back by Saturday at three.'

'Saturday at three? Sounds familiar. Have I an important appointment, Mrs Allerton?' He feigned a frown.

'Mmm, very important, Mr McCabe.' Her lips ran lightly over his chin.

'I'll be there, Caro. With bells on,' he told her. 'Even if I have to swim the Pacific.'

That last week seemed impossibly shorter than the previous ones, and so much happened Carolyn felt her head was spinning. Suzy arrived to help with the final arrangements and set to organising with a will. She was full of excitement because she had found Carolyn and Leith a house. Some friends of hers were going to be spending six months in Canada and wanted tenants for their home for that time.

'It would be a great solution,' she enthused. 'Your flat's

a bit small for the three of you and you need time to find the right place to settle. You'll have six whole months to look at the properties on the market. Bill and Kathy need reliable people to house-sit so,' she shrugged, 'everybody's happy.'

With that she whisked Carolyn and Bodie off to meet her friends and to see the house. Carolyn loved it. It was a rambling ranch-style house with a pool and barbecue area at the back, and it was set on two tree-studded acres. Best of all, it was only ten minutes' drive further out from where they now lived. It was ideal.

Bodie gazed about him in awe. 'Mum, this is totally decadent!' He turned with a huge grin. 'But I love it.'

Suzy insisted they rang Leith and as he was familiar with the house he agreed it would solve the problem of where they were going to live. So that meant a hectic couple of days shifting their things from the flat to the new house so that they would be able to move straight in when they returned from their honeymoon. They were only having three days at the Coast, but after the New Year they were planning a month in the Caribbean.

Suzy had everything running like clockwork until they had a call from Dave McCabe in the States to tell them their mother had slipped over in a department store and broken her wrist. She was badly shaken up and they had been unable to catch their plane back to Australia. Now they wouldn't be arriving until after the wedding.

Suzy groaned with disappointment. 'Mum will be so annoyed with herself!'

'Perhaps we should postpone the wedding,' Carolyn began numbly.

'Heavens, no!' Suzy assured her. 'Dave said Mum was adamant about not altering the plans. Now that Leith's finally marrying she doesn't want anything changing his mind.'

On Friday Leith phoned from the airport. 'I know it's supposed to be bad luck for the groom to see the bride the day before the wedding, but I'd dearly love to hold you in my arms right now,' he said huskily. 'I keep thinking about having your beautiful body close to mine and I'm quietly going out of my mind.'

The sound of his voice had the same fire coursing along Carolyn's veins. 'Me, too,' she breathed. 'Maybe it was all fantasy. Do you think we could have had the same erotic dreams?'

'The most fantastic erotic dreams of my life,' he chuckled. 'Roll on tomorrow night and we'll put those particular dreams on replay, in full living colour!'

Carolyn's fingers tightened on the receiver. 'I love you,' she said shakily.

'I won't believe it until I get you to myself and you can show me,' Leith teased. 'A crowded airport is not the place for this type of conversation. I'm going to have to think pure thoughts for a while before I walk away.' He laughed ruefully, and the deep vibrant sound made Carolyn wish she could reach out and touch him, have him assuage the ache inside her that turned her legs to water.

'Did . . . did everything go all right with Peter Kruger?' she asked tentatively.

'Yes, eventually.' He went on to explain just what the vengeful Peter Kruger had been up to. 'I only hope we can keep it from his father. Kruger's a fool,' Leith said shortly. 'But enough of that. How's Bodie? A celebrity now he's had his photograph in the newspaper?'

Carolyn smiled. 'He was pretty thrilled about that. The reporters did a very good write-up on his successes at the Games in Melbourne and in the Sprint Championships here in Brisbane. He's dying to show you, so expect it at the reception if he doesn't drag out his clippings during the ceremony.'

Leith laughed.

'Bodie's very happy we're getting married. And so am

I.' Carolyn paused, her face flushing. 'No second thoughts?'

'None,' he replied firmly. 'Roll on Saturday! And Saturday night.'

Carolyn's heartbeats were skipping erratically at the deep throb in Leith's voice. 'Have you heard any more about your mother?' she asked unevenly, reluctantly changing the subject.

'I spoke to her last night. She's had her wrist set and she's absolutely livid she can't be here for the wedding. But they'll be back by the time we return from the coast.' His voice dropped silkily. 'I wish we were down there now.'

Carolyn's laugh caught in her throat. 'What might we be doing?' she teased shamelessly.

'Do I have to tell you?' He groaned. 'And you can guess what you're doing to me now!'

'Mmm,' she murmured.

'Caro, you're a witch. I'll get my revenge tomorrow night.'

'I can hardly wait!' she chuckled softly.

'So brave on the other end of the phone. We'll see tomorrow,' he threatened lightly. 'Here's my driver so I'll have to go. And Caro,' his voice dropped again, 'don't be late.'

'No more than five minutes,' she promised huskily.

She slowly replaced the receiver and smiled to herself. Tomorrow afternoon she would become Mrs Leith McCabe. She took a deep steadying breath and closed her eyes. And please God, he would never find out about Carol Barton.

'Admit it, Leith McCabe. You lulled me into a false sense of security in the first couple of sets, didn't you?' Carolyn teased as they entered their unit.

'Would I do that?' He raised one eyebrow and she laughed easily.

'Be warned for next time that I'm on to your sneaky tactics!' She wiped her armband over her forehead. 'I feel all hot and sticky, I think I'll have a quick shower before lunch.'

Leith was slipping their tennis bag into the small hall cupboard and she ran her eyes over the length of him as he bent over. A tiny shiver ran down her spine as she recalled his firm smooth body moving with hers the evening before and again that morning. His lovemaking had been all that she remembered it was, all and more, so much, much more. She fought the urge to cross to him, to wrap her arms around him, but she hesitated, turning away, walking down the short hallway to their bedroom.

She kicked off her sneakers and stepped out of the shorts and T-shirt she had worn to play tennis and padded barefooted into the adjacent bathroom. Turning on the shower-spray, she shed her bra and pants. Her hand went out to test the temperature of the water and as she stepped into the large cubicle a light finger ran provocatively down the length of her spine, sending spirals of pleasure along its naked length.

She caught her breath and turned slightly, her face flushing as Leith's bright eyes ran over the contours of her body. And he was as naked as she was. Her eyes met and held his.

'I could do with a shower, too,' he said softly. 'A long one.' He followed her into the shower recess. 'And something tells me we won't be conserving any water.'

His arm reached behind her for the scented soap and her gaze dropped to the broad expanse of his chest, was held fascinated by the pearly droplets of water that clung to the soft dark hair curling there. She watched a small rivulet trickle downwards, gathering momentum as it coursed over the flatness of his stomach, skirting his navel to speed lower, and her mouth went suddenly dry at the totally male beauty of him.

'Beautiful!'

Carolyn imagined she had said the word, but it was Leith voicing her thoughts and she dragged her eyes upwards to find his own gaze resting on her breasts. Her nipples tensed, thrusting towards him.

'You are unbelievably beautiful, Mrs McCabe,' he repeated thickly, and his wet hands slid over her hips, her ribcage, to cup her breasts.

Carolyn swayed forwards at the same moment as he did and their bodies touched, blended together. His hands moved around her so that her breasts were pressed against his chest and his lips seared a fiery trail across her forehead to rest on her temples over the erratic throb of her pulse.

She became aware of his soapy hands on her back, sliding sensuously over her shoulder blades, lingering tantalisingly along the slight hollow of her spine before making a circular motion around her hips, her buttocks, pressing her deliriously against the hardness of his arousal. Her hands luxuriated in the smooth dampness of his shoulders, clutching at his firm skin as his fingers continued their inciting trail over her tingling body.

Her lips caressed his shoulder, rose to rain quick enraptured kisses along the curve of his neck and she tasted the faint saltiness of his skin.

Leith's hands came to rest on her hips and he drew slightly away from her. Carolyn protested deep in her throat, but he was merely turning her around, fitting his long body into the curve of her back as his hands cupped her breats again, smoothing the soft fragrant soap over their fulness, sending curls of desire arrowing downwards to erupt in waves of wanting in the pit of her stomach.

His fingers circled and teased the taut twin peaks of her nipples until she gasped out his name, turning her head so that her questing lips found his cheek, the line of his jaw. He shifted slightly so that their lips met beneath the fine crystal spray and they kissed recklessly, quick agitated enflamed kisses.

Leith caught her lip lightly between his teeth and then

traced its wet outline with his tongue-tip as his hands slid over the flatness of her stomach, downwards, his hands separating to mould the tops of her thighs. As his fingers sought out each secret sensorial place Carolyn moaned her pleasure, her body clamouring for the complete fulfilment she knew he could give her.

When his fingers stilled she moved sensually against him, the firmness of her buttocks pressed against him making him catch his breath. He turned her around to face him, holding her away from him, and she could see the tight control he had on himself. He was as aroused as she was and the blazing fire in his blue eyes almost had her legs giving way beneath her.

Drawing a ragged breath, he lifted her hand and placed the cake of soap in it. 'Now it's your turn,' he said, his voice deeply uneven.

Carolyn foamed the soap between her palms and then smoothed them over the contours of his chest, the breadth of his shoulders, his hard flat midriff, lower over his stomach, one finger circling, flicking into his navel, lower. Her fingers faltered, changed direction, slid over his hips, down his muscular thighs, back over his hips, returning to his stomach, faltered again. Then Leith's hands covered hers, guiding them downwards, and she heard him catch his breath, murmur deep in his chest.

He pulled her hard against him, his lips claiming hers, passion seizing them both, swirling upwards, lifting them higher as the warm jets of the shower-spray cascaded over them, washing the fragrant bubbles of soap from their bodies.

Leith's kisses drugged her as his lips found the throbbing pulse at the base of her throat, seared downwards over her breasts, taking each aroused bud in his mouth. Carolyn's senses careered out of control as her hands moved over him. His arms came around her, lifting her, and he stepped from the shower. Then they were together on the bed and she turned to him, clutching him to her in feverish desperation. She wanted him so badly she was sure an earthquake couldn't have stopped them as they surged together, racing passionately to the climax of mutual ecstasy that seemed to Carolyn to last for ever.

She knew she was floating, drifting somewhere high up on a plane where only Leith could take her, a place she never dreamed existed. Before Leith. A faint fulfilled sigh escaped her lips, teasing the skin of his shoulder and his hand moved lingeringly over her breasts, her stomach, to settle possessively on the curve of her hip.

Carolyn lifted her head and looked into the deep dark blue of his eyes. This close she could see the fine tiny lines radiating from the corners of his eyes, the darkening shadow of his beard, the creases in his cheeks that deepened so attractively when he smiled. They deepened now, the corners of his mouth lifting. His mouth. Her gaze settled momentarily on his lips, feeling again the spark of the fire his lips could create within her. Her eyes met his again. God, how she loved him! Did he know just how much?

'You are really something, Mrs McCabe. Do you know that?' he said softly. He lifted his hand, one finger lightly tracing the arch of each eyebrow, the line of her small nose, the curve of her lips still slightly swollen from his kisses. 'So cool and composed on the outside.' His fingertip slid between her lips and she held it gently between her teeth. 'But who could guess at the smouldering fire on the inside?'

Carolyn flushed. 'I didn't know it could be like that,' she told him softly, and she could feel his eyes on her face as she watched her own fingers twisting the dark swirls of hair on his chest. 'I've never . . . I love you so much, Leith.' She couldn't hold back the words that were suddenly inadequate to express her feelings for him.

He shifted slightly, resting his head on his hand so that

he was looking down at her. 'Tell me about Bodie's father.'

The question took her completely by surprise, felt almost like a blow, even though his tone was soft. Her eyes searched his face but she could find no resentment there.

'I was very young, barely sixteen,' she began huskily. 'He wasn't much older. He was the first person in my life to take any notice of me, to make me feel special, I suppose.' She looked up at him. 'I loved him for that. Now I can barely remember his face. It seems another world ago.' She swallowed. 'He died before Bodie was born.'

Leith's hand gently cupped her breast. 'You never considered giving Bodie up?'

Carolyn nodded. 'Before he was born I had decided to have him adopted. My parents didn't want me around when they found out I was pregnant, so they sent me up here to my aunt. She was a very sensible, realistic woman. We sat down and we discussed it and I decided adoption would be for the best.'

Leith raised his eyebrows.

'But when he was born and I held him——' she shook her head, 'I just couldn't part with him. My aunt didn't try to change my mind. She simply stated the facts of my responsibility to Bodie and let me get on with it. She looked after him when I went to college and collected him from school when I began working for Kruger's. I wouldn't have managed without her.' Carolyn sighed. 'Aunt Josie pointed out the importance of giving Bodie a stable life, and that meant no long line of men-friends. In the beginning I was too busy studying to give a social life a thought and later,' she shrugged, 'there was no one until you.'

Leith raised her hand to his lips and kissed each finger, gently rubbing the bright golden band of her wedding-ring. Then he drew her into his arms, kissing her tenderly, holding her against him. Sudden tears welled up in Carolyn's eyes, squeezing between her closed lashes as a wave of pure love for him grasped her entire body. Her hands tightened about him as fear clutched at her. How fragile their future was. If he found out——

'Hey!' His lips broke from their kiss and he laughed softly, his thumb brushing the tears from her cheeks. 'Happy tears, I hope. Carolyn, you're the very best thing that's ever happened to me in my life,' he said simply and sincerely.

They lay in each other's arms, content to be together, and Carolyn ran her hand lightly over his thigh. Leith murmured softly, a rueful arousing sound.

'Have a heart, Mrs McCabe! As much as I'd like to repeat the last hour you'll have to forgive me just now. I haven't quite got my second breath.'

Carolyn saw the sensual amusement in his eyes and her lips curled upwards. 'Don't tell me you're getting old, Mr McCabe,' she teased and he pulled a grieved face.

'I think I'm going to age very quickly from now on,' he said with a mock frown.

She laughed and then sobered. 'Young or old, I love you, Leith McCabe,' she said seriously.

His hand pulled her head down on to the curve of his shoulder. 'And I love you, too, Caro,' he said softly.

They must have slept, for Carolyn was started awake by the sound of the telephone jangling in the hall.

'I'll get it.' Leith slipped his arm from beneath her head and slid off the bed. 'Don't move an inch, Mrs McCabe.' He bent over to brush her breast with his lips. 'I think I may have found that second breath I thought I'd lost!'

Carolyn smiled as she watched his long naked body stride out of the room. She stretched contentedly and burrowed her head into the pillow. When she awoke again the sun was low in the sky and the bedroom was in shadow. Her hand automatically reached for Leith, but she was alone in the bed.

Standing up, she pulled on her towelling robe and walked on bare feet through to the sitting-room. At first she didn't see him, but his slight movement caught her eye and she crossed to the balcony.

He had his back to her, his elbows resting on the railings as he gazed out over the panorama of the beaches, Coolangatta, the pines on top of Greenmount Hill, the peaceful curve of Rainbow Bay below them, the projecting jut of Point Danger. He was wearing a pair of denim shorts and Carolyn moved up behind him, wrapping her arms around him, resting her cheek on his warm back. She thought she felt him tense momentarily, but then he relaxed and she let her lips trail over his shoulder, reaching around to kiss his cheek.

'I must have dozed off. Why didn't you wake me, darling?'

There was a strangely strained pause before he replied. 'I hadn't the heart,' he said evenly. 'You looked so peacefully dead to the world.'

Carolyn leaned against him, her arm still lightly around him. 'Mmm!' She drew a deep breath. 'This view is fantastic. The water's so blue.' She nuzzled his shoulder. 'Who was on the phone?'

'Dad,' he said quietly. 'They arrived home today, but Mum's a little tired from the trip. They'll be coming up to Brisbane at the end of the week.'

'Oh.' If Suzy hadn't recognised her then why should Leith's parents? Carolyn ran her tongue-tip over his shoulder and the lapel of her bathrobe fell open to expose one creamy breast. Leith's eyes were drawn downwards, his gaze brilliantly intense. 'I hope they'll like me.,

His hand reached out to widen the opening of her robe, his fingers sliding over her smooth skin.

Carolyn caught her breath. 'What were you saying about second breath?' she asked lightly, her eyes dancing.

Leith held her gaze and something in the blue depths of his eyes made the smile fade from her lips.

'Leith?'

He blinked and stood upright, his hand moving now on her breast. 'I did, didn't I?' he said flatly, and picking her up carried her into the sitting-room and lowered her to the soft pile of the carpet. His lips claimed hers punishingly, his fingers bruising so that she protested, her heart filled with a fearful dread. His lovemaking had changed. Gone was the tender lover. Now it was as though he was a man driven by anger, and she cried out as his hard body moved over hers.

Poised above her, his eyes locked with hers. In the few seconds before his lashes fell to shield their expression Carolyn thought she saw pain in their deep blueness. Then he lowered his lips to hers, gentler now, and soon everything was wiped from her mind except Leith and the sound of their bodies moving together.

That night she lay awake beside him long after he had fallen asleep, and in the morning he was up and dressed before she awoke. They spent the morning on the beach and for most of the time Leith left her to body-surf out in the curling waves. She wanted to surf with him, but she lay sunbathing beneath a striped unbrella, sensing that he wanted to be alone.

After lunch they left for Brisbane. The new house was as beautiful as Carolyn remembered it was, but somehow the shine of moving in with Leith had dulled just a little. He stood beside her gazing expressionlessly at the house for a few moments before silently picking up their cases and leading the way up to the front door.

Carolyn went through to the kitchen and set out two coffee-mugs on the bright lime-green counter-top. She plugged in the percolator.

Leith had disappeared into the shower and she longed to go to him but she held herself back. From those few moments on the unit's balcony yesterday afternoon she knew she had lost a part of the man she had married. The change in him was so painfully obvious.

She bit her lip. Was he tired of her already? She ran a shaky hand over her brow and then stilled as a thought she had been keeping religiously at bay broke its shackles and brought the cold hand of fear clutching at her heart. Had he found out?

That's ridiculous, she chided herself. How could he have done that? Who would have told him? They had been alone since their wedding.

Leith walked into the kitchen knotting his tie. 'No coffee for me,' he said evenly. 'When's Bodie coming home?'

'When I phone Joy to tell her we're back,' Carolyn replied, yearning for him to take her in his arms.

'I have to go in to the office,' he said, not looking at her as he checked in his pocket for his wallet.

'The office? But——'

'I won't be long, a couple of hours at the most.' His hands reached out, lingering on her arms for a moment before he pulled her lightly against him. 'I'll see you later.' He kissed her once, a hard quick kiss, and then he was gone.

Carolyn stood where he'd left her, unable to move. He was keeping something from her and she had a dreadful premonition she knew what it was.

Compelled, she walked through to the luxurious living-room, down the thickly carpeted hallway to one of the spare bedrooms where she had stored boxes of her things they wouldn't need to unpack while they lived here. She knew exactly which box to open to pull out a pile of books, and then the photo album Bodie had been looking at such short weeks ago. Finding the page she gazed down at the group of teenagers.

Three girls and four boys. Kathy and Don. Janie and Pete. Terry and herself. And Chris. Tall, fair-haired and good looking Chris McCabe who at seventeen so much resembled his sister Suzy. Chris had the biggest motorbike and plenty of money to spend. Pete had brought him along to their group. Heaven knows where they'd met, for it was so obvious their backgrounds were poles apart.

Right from that first day Chris had made it plain that he fancied Carolyn. And from fourteen years on Carolyn could admit she had been flattered. The familiar wave of guilt surged to the surface.

She searched Chris's face in the photograph for any resemblance to Leith, but she could see none. Perhaps something about the eyes. But Chris's had been fair while Leith was dark. And Chris's good looks had been youthfully unformed, more regular, not having the angular ruggedness of his brother's features.

Of course Terry had not been impressed by the newcomer paying Carolyn so much attention and he had warned Chris off in no uncertain terms. Carolyn was his girl. It had gone on for a couple of weeks until it culminated in the final fateful scene one afternoon in a Melbourne back street.

Had she really encouraged Chris? Carolyn instinctively shook her head. She hadn't meant to, but Chris had been so persistent and it was a novelty to have two good-looking boys vying for her attention.

That afternoon the boys had been working on their bikes in a vacant allotment. Chris wanted to take his machine out for a test run and he offered to take Carolyn with him. Terry grabbed Chris's shirt-front and angrily told him to back off. One thing led to another until Chris turned to Carolyn and asked her to make up her own mind.

'She stays with me,' growled Terry. 'She wants no part of any spoilt little rich boy. What are you doing down here anyway, McCabe? Slumming? Why don't you go back to your toffee-nosed family and buy yourself a débutante?'

Chris lunged at Terry and they sprawled on the footpath. Carolyn appealed to Pete to stop them, but he shook his head, saying the fight had been brewing for weeks. The two boys struggled to their feet, landing punches on each other. Carolyn tried to intervene, but they pushed her aside and she would have fallen if Pete hadn't caught her.

Then Chris swung a hard right that connected with Terry's jaw and Terry overbalanced, falling backwards, hitting his head on the cement kerb with a sickening thud. He lay still. No one moved for immeasurable seconds as they gazed in horror at Terry's limp body. Chris was drawing rasping breaths as Pete slowly bent down.

'He's not breathing,' he said thinly. 'I think he's dead.'

'He can't be dead!' declared Chris, his voice high with stunned shock.

Carolyn flung herself down beside Terry feeling frantically for some sign of life. 'I can't find his pulse.'

'He can't be dead,' Kathy repeated, crouching down, lifting his other limp hand. 'We'd better get an ambulance.'

'I think he is dead. God, what'll we do?' Pete stepped backwards. 'The cops will come—I don't want to get mixed up with them again.'

'He can't be dead!' Carolyn cried hysterically, shaking Terry's shoulder. 'He can't be!'

'He is, Carol—he is, I tell you!' Pete turned to Chris, who stood white-faced. 'You'd better vanish, mate. They're gonna say you killed him.'

'But it was just a fight, an accident!' Chris's voice rose in panic.

'You hit him,' Pete reminded him.

'And now he's dead. ' Carolyn looked up, tears coursing down her cheeks.

Chris stood almost blankly looking down at Terry's body and then he turned and ran to his bike, kicking it started, roaring off along the street, leaving his crash-helmet behind on the ground. Ten minutes later on the freeway as Chris pushed his bike to the limit he sideswiped a car and crashed into the guide-rail, dying instantly of massive head injuries.

The telephone rang and Carolyn was startled back to the present with a jolt that had the photo album falling from her nerveless fingers to the floor. She replaced it in the carton and like a robot she walked into the study and lifted the receiver.

'Mum? Hi. Welcome back.' Bodie's familiar voice brought tears back to her eyes.

'Oh, Bodie! How are you, love?'

'I'm fine. Did you and Leith have a good time down at the beach?'

'Yes. Yes, we did.' Carolyn's fingers tightened on the receiver. 'But it's nice to be back.' She fought to keep her voice even.

'You mean you prefer the suburbs to the sand and surf? That I don't believe!' Bodie laughed.

'Well——' Carolyn tried to laugh with him.

'Brett and I are just off to training, so is it okay if I get Mrs Conlon to drop me at home afterwards?'

'Of course love. I'm looking forward to seeing you.' Carolyn swallowed, suddenly wanting the normality of just Bodie and herself and no heavy weight over her heart at the thought of losing Leith.

'Me, too. Is Leith there?' Bodie was asking.

'No. Yes. I mean, he's . . . he's in the shower.' Carolyn couldn't believe she'd lied to Bodie. Why had she done so? To protect her son? Or herself?

'Oh. Okay, I'll see you both after training then. Bye, Mum.'

'Yes. Goodbye, love.' Carolyn walked through to the lounge and sank into a deep chair, tucking her legs up under her, wrapping her arms protectively around her.

What was she to do? She just couldn't think properly. Where was the calm controlled unflappable Carolyn Allerton? McCabe, she corrected herself. Although for how long she didn't know.

Would that be Leith's solution? To end their marriage after a few short days?

She sat there, unaware of the passage of time, until the bang of a car door filtered through to her and she struggled to her feet, realising the room had darkened. As the sound of footsteps crossed the verandah she ran her hand nervously over her tousled hair. Maybe it would be Bodie, she told herself, knowing all the while that it was Leith.

He paused as he entered the living-room his eyes going to her as she got shakily to her feet. Quite unconsciously she registered that the creases in his cheeks seemed to be etched a little deeper, that his blue eyes gleamed starkly from his tensed, pale face.

She began to turn from him, but without a word he crossed to her, his fingers biting into her arm as he brought her relentlessly around to face him, so that his eyes blazed down into her drawn features. His gaze held her captive, as fatally fascinated as a moth by a flame.

In his other hand he grasped a sheaf of photocopies and he held the top one up, comparing a sixteen-year-old's face to Carolyn's. He drew a sharp breath.

Carolyn was incapable of uttering a sound. This was the moment she had been dreading yet now she was strangely numb, almost resigned.

'Why didn't you tell me?' he bit out, his words coldly chipped, his lips a thin tight line.

CHAPTER TEN

CAROLYN shook her head. 'What . . . what could I say?' she asked flatly. 'I tried to tell you. That afternoon in your apartment in Melbourne. But I . . . I just couldn't. I loved you so much I didn't want to lose you.'

His fingers tightened and Carolyn flinched.

'You're hurting me, Leith!'

'God, I could kill you!' A flash of pain crossed her face. 'Surely you knew I'd find out eventually?'

'I hoped you wouldn't. No one knew about it and it was all a long time ago. I——' She shook her head.

Leith swore softly, releasing her so abruptly that she stumbled backwards and had to grasp the chair for support. 'I'm sorry,' she whispered, her eyes on his tense back.

He ran a hand around the back of his neck. 'And that makes it all right?'

'How did you find out?' Her voice was a hoarse murmur, but he turned around to face her, tossing the photocopies of the newspaper reports on the chair. His hands went aggressively to his hips and his mouth twisted mockingly.

'My father recognised you from the wedding photos Suzy took, the polaroid ones.'

'Then your family all know?' Carolyn said flatly.

'Yes.'

'Your father told you when he rang the unit yesterday?' The pieces all fell into place as Leith nodded. 'Then you knew that afternoon when——'

'When we made love?' he finished bitterly. 'I knew it was a possibility, although I couldn't bring Carol Barton's face to mind. Does that shock you, my darling wife? That suspecting who you were I still couldn't leave you alone?' His lips twisted self-derogatorily. 'Well, let me shock you a little more, Caro. Even now, knowing who you are, I could——'

He turned abruptly away to lean his hands on the bookcase, his back to her once more.

Carolyn picked up the photocopies in numbed fingers. 'You collected all this, in less than twenty-four hours?'

'Being able to pay handsomely has its advantages,' he remarked cynically as he faced her again. 'I had someone go out to see your mother.'

'My mother?' she breathed.

'Your mother was more than willing to tell all. How your stepfather never legally adopted you and that you had no right to the name Barton. That you'd shamed them and been packed off to Queensland. She delighted in reporting that you had reverted to your father's name—Allerton.'

'Leith, I had nothing to do with your brother's death please believe me. I didn't want it to end like that. I was flattered that Chris found me attractive, but,' she shook her head, 'I would have given anything to have turned back the clock that day. But I couldn't.'

Her eyes pleaded with him, but his anger hadn't abated. His gaze held hers coldly, impaling, searing down into her very soul.

'I still can't believe you could have changed so much.'

'I haven't changed, Leith,' she said quietly, 'just grown older, like you have, and hopefully I've learned from the mistakes of my youth.' She shook her head. 'Believe me, I've paid dearly for them over the years as far as my peace of mind goes. Do you think I haven't been eaten away with guilt for my part in that dreadful day? Bodie knows nothing about it, so do you think I haven't lived in terror of someone recognising me and having him find out the whole sordid story?' She drew a ragged breath. 'Since he started showing so much promise as a swimmer

I've guarded him against publicity as much as I could. That article in the paper before we were married is only the second time his photo has been featured. And I've never allowed any personal details to be made public. I don't want him to——'

The sound of a car pulling up in the drive had her swinging away, her words catching in her throat. 'It's Bodie,' she breathed, and she turned back to Leith, her hand going unconsciously out to him. 'Please, Leith, this has nothing to do with him——'

'Hasn't it, Carolyn?' he asked harshly.

'No. No, please, Leith. Don't take it out on him. I don't want him hurt.' Her voice broke, her eyes pleading with him as she blinked back the tears.

He stood before her seemingly unmoved, his face set and expressionless. As Bodie's steps bounded across the verandah Carolyn thrust the newspaper clippings into her pocket. And then the door swung open.

'Mum—Leith—welcome back! It's great to see you.' He grinned from ear to ear as he folded his mother in a bearhug.

Carolyn clutched him desperately to her, feeling his hard young body, smelling the faint aroma of chlorine that still clung to his damp hair. Bodie groaned exaggeratedly.

'Hey, Mum, you're squeezing me to death! Didn't miss me that much, did you?' he asked, and she reluctantly released him, forcing a light laugh.

'Yes, I did,' she said a little huskily.

Bodie laughed too and then turned to Leith. 'Did you have a good time?' When he realised what he'd said he blushed.

Leith moved then and his smile was even more forced than Carolyn's. 'Sure did. And we were just trying to decide where to have dinner, a restaurant or perhaps the Pizza Hut. What would you like?'

'The Pizza Hut.' Bodie's eyes lit up. 'Haven't had a pizza for ages.'

'Right. Put your bag in your room and we'll go.'

Bodie ran down the hallway.

'Thank you,' Carolyn said softly when he was out of earshot.

'For what?' Leith bit out. 'Do you think I want to be the one to crush Bodie's image of his perfect mother?' He walked towards the door. 'I'll wait in the car.'

Afterwards Carolyn couldn't have told how she got through that meal, but she did, and somehow both she and Leith managed to show no outward signs of their antagonism in front of Bodie, although once or twice she saw Bodie dart a quick puzzled look from Leith to herself.

When they arrived back home Bodie left them to do his homework and Carolyn stood looking at Leith.

'We have to talk,' she began, but Leith turned away.

'I have some work to do. Don't wait up for me,' he said flatly, and disappeared into his study.

Carolyn spent a wretched evening trying to read, and after Bodie had gone to bed she took a cup of coffee through to Leith, tapping tentatively on the door before going inside. He accepted the cup without looking up.

'I . . . I'm going to bed now,' she ventured. 'Will you be long?'

His eyes rose to meet hers then and she thought she saw a shadow of fire in his expression before he lowered his gaze to his papers. 'Hours yet.'

Carolyn stood waiting for him to say something else, but when he didn't she slowly left him. Did he expect her to sleep in the main bedroom or move into a guest-room? She looked at the huge double bed and went through to the bathroom to have a shower. By ten o'clock her eyelids were drooping, but Leith hadn't joined her by the time she fell asleep and when she awoke in the morning his pillow was undisturbed.

Heavy-eyed, she dragged herself out of bed and dressed hurriedly. She'd overslept and she had to get Bodie up and drive him to training. His room was empty and she found him sharing tea and toast with Leith in the kitchen.

'You needn't have got up, Mum. Leith's taking me to training this morning.' Bodie put his last piece of toast into his mouth.

'You don't have to do that.' Carolyn turned to Leith, fighting down a painful urge to wrap her arms around him and beg him not to treat her as though she weren't there.

'I want to get in to work early.' He turned from her and shrugged his arms into his suit jacket. 'I've arranged to have your new car delivered today, so you'll have it to collect Bodie this evening.'

'New car? But what about my own car?' Their old Gemini was parked rather forlornly in the huge garage next to the Jaguar.

'They'll take it away when they deliver the new one,' Leith replied expressionlessly.

'That Gemini deserves a medal for perserverence!' laughed Bodie. 'What sort did you get Mum, Leith?'

'A BMW. But you can change if it you don't like it,' he told the wall above Carolyn's head.

'If she doesn't like it?' Bodie repeated incredulously. 'She'll love it! They're really well—elegant.' He looked at Leith with open adoration. 'Thanks, Leith!'

Carolyn pulled herself together. 'Yes, Thank you, Leith. I didn't expect you to . . .'

But Leith had turned away, striding towards the door.

'If the car hasn't been delivered by lunch-time ring Maggie and leave a message for me and I'll see to it.'

In other words, he didn't want to talk to her, not even on the phone. Oh, Leith, her heart contracted painfully, what can I do to make it right again, to make you love me like you did for those few short weeks?

Carolyn was preparing dinner before collecting Bodie from training when the phone rang.

'Carolyn? I'm glad I caught you.' Leith's voice, deep and resonant, sounding more like the Leith she'd married, had her leaning weakly against the kitchen wall. 'I wanted to let you know not to wait dinner for me. There's some trouble down in Hobart I have to attend to and I'm flying down tonight.'

'Tonight? But your clothes——' Carolyn began, her heart sinking.

'I'm stopping off in Melbourne, so I'll call at the flat and collect what I need,' he said evenly.

'When will you be back?' Her knuckles were white where she clutched the phone.

'Probably Thursday. I'll see you then.' There was a buzz of a broken connection and it was some time before she slowly replaced the receiver on its cradle.

She woke to the sensation of having been disturbed but couldn't identify the sound that had drawn her from her light sleep. Blinking she peered into the semi-darkness. The full moon shone through the open curtains and the definite click of a closing door had her sitting bolt upright.

With a shaky hand she reached out and flicked on the bedside lamp, finding some comfort in the soft glow. There was someone in the living-room. Perhaps Bodie was getting himself a glass of milk.

Throwing back the light bedcovers, she padded on bare feet to the bedroom door, easing it silently open. A dark figure loomed largely in the hallway and as she formulated a scream a deep voice said quickly, 'It's me, Carolyn.'

She felt her knees almost give way beneath her as she clutched at the door frame.

'I'm sorry I frightened you,' Leith continued quietly, 'but I was trying not to wake you.'

'That's all right. I just didn't expect you back until tomorrow. I thought you were a burglar.' She walked shakily over to the bed and sat down, realising too late that she hadn't slipped on her robe and that the subdued light from the lamp rendered her short nightdress virtually transparent.

Leith entered the bedroom and tossed his suit jacket on to the chair, his fingers removing his tie. Even in the dim light Carolyn could see the lines of tiredness bracketing his mouth and she glanced at the clock. One-thirty.

'Did everything go off all right in Hobart?' she asked tentatively.

He nodded. 'I cleared it up the first day. Then I flew up to Airlie Beach.'

'You look tired.' She yearned to cross to him, massage his neck, but his whole stance did not encourage any intimacies.

'I am a little tired,' he replied. 'I've been working on some revised plans for a couple of Kruger's other projects.' He flexed his shoulders. 'I could use a shower.'

Immediately Carolyn's thoughts went to the shower they'd shared at the Coast so few days ago and a yearning sensation began low in her stomach sending shivery signals upwards, and she swallowed as her nipples tensed, plainly obvious through the thin material of her nightdress.

Leith's eyes were shuttered by his lashes, but she felt his gaze burning over her, as enflaming as his fiery physical touch. His fingers paused as he unbuttoned his shirt and then he slowly pulled the shirt from the waistband of his trousers.

Carolyn's breathing quickened with her heartbeats. 'Did you have a meal?'

'I ate at the airport,' he replied flatly.

'Shall I make you something to eat, some coffee?' she asked and he turned from her to toss his shirt on the chair with his coat.

The hard muscles of his arms and shoulders were highlighted in the semi-shadows and Carolyn watched almost mesmerised as he moved.

'I wouldn't mind some coffee,' he said as he walked towards their bathroom. He left the door open and the harsh light streamed into the bedroom.

Carolyn stood up then, hurriedly slipping into her terry-towelling robe before walking quietly past Bodie's room to the kitchen. She quickly made some toasted sandwiches and was pouring the coffee into two mugs when she sensed Leith behind her.

He had shaved and his hair was still damp from his shower, and he had never looked more potently attractive. He wore only his robe and he had thrust his hands into its deep pockets.

'I've made you a snack.' She crossed to keep the counter-top between them, but only after her eyes had moved upwards from his bare brown legs to the curling hair on his chest where the lapels of his robe fell open. Had he seen her unconscious scrutiny? He must have. Her cheeks burned with embarrassment.

Leith sat down at the breakfast bar and ate the sandwiches she had made before relaxing back with his coffee. 'Thanks. I must have been hungry. And airport meals are never exactly cordon bleu.'

'Leith, about the car, the BMW,' Carolyn began. 'I can't accept it, it's far too expensive.

'Isn't it expected?' He looked across at her, his lips twisting. 'I'm a wealthy man, so shouldn't my wife have a car comparable with her change of circumstances?'

Wordlessly she shook her head.

'Well, Carolyn, shouldn't she?'

'Your wealth wasn't the reason I married you, if that's what you're implying. How could you believe that?'

He gave a mirthless laugh. 'But you have to admit it helped you decide to take me on.'

'That's ridiculous!' Carolyn threw back at him.

'Is it?'

'Yes, it is, and you know it is.' Her voice caught on a sob and she brushed past him, running down the long hallway into the sanctuary of the bedroom. She leant on the dressing-table fighting back her tears. How could he think that of her?

The door behind her opened, but she remained where she was, not allowing herself to face him even as the door closed.

'Do you want a divorce?' she asked flatly.

'There'll be no divorce,' he replied with cold finality. 'At least not yet.'

Carolyn turned then to stare dry-eyed at him. He was leaning easily back against the door, his arms folded, watching her through lash-shrouded eyes.

'I don't intend to have the gossiping tongues starting on me or my family. They'd have a field day. A marriage lasting less than a week!' He gave a bitter laugh. 'Something of a record, wouldn't you say, Carolyn?'

She remained silent as something deep inside her died a painful death.

'Oh, no. We'll stay married for an acceptable time.'

'And what do you consider to be an acceptable time?' she asked, feeling as though her whole world had fallen right in on top of her.

'Who knows?' he shrugged. 'Until I'm ready.' He watched her arrogantly from across the room.

'Oh, Leith, please! Don't do this to us!' Carolyn breathed, and he smiled sardonically.

'I haven't done anything, Carolyn.'

She gazed at him impotently and then shook her head, at the hard inflexibility in his expression, the lack of even the faintest shadow of compassion or the sign that he might relent. She passed a shaky hand over her eyes.

'I'm tired, Leith. I'll use the bedroom across the hall and tomorrow I'll move my things.'

'I think not, Carolyn. You're still my wife, and I intend

that you'll stay right here until I choose to change the situation.'

Her whole body tensed and then of its own accord she felt the first stirrings of a response at the implication of his words.

'Oh, I shan't ask any more than the price you were originally willing to pay.' The smile on his face chilled her to the bone, and she wrapped her arms protectively about herself.

'Exactly what do you mean by that?' Her voice was little more than a hoarse whisper as her throat closed.

'What do you think I mean, Mrs McCabe?'

Carolyn could only shake her head.

Leith's eyes roved almost insolently over her body, settling on the thrusting curve of her breasts, before sliding meaningfully in the direction of the large double bed.

Her hand crept to her throat. 'No.' The word broke from her in a ragged expulsion of breath.

'No?' Leith raised one fine dark eyebrow. 'I say yes, my dear deceiving wife.' He pushed himself away from the door with one lithe movement and walked purposefully towards her.

Carolyn's shaky legs carried her backwards until she bumped up against the bed. She attempted to ward him off, but he reached for her, his own hands evading hers with overpowering ease, propelling her towards him until her body was moulded to the solid length of his.

'Leith, don't——' Her words were lost as his lips came swooping down to claim hers, kissing her savagely, bruising the soft inner tissue of her mouth. Her hands pushed ineffectually against him but she was no match for his powerful strength. The kiss lasted for long blazing seconds and when his lips surrendered hers they were both breathing as though they had run a marathon.

A tear overflowed to course down Carolyn's cheek and for a moment she thought the pain in her eyes had reached him, that he would release her, put an end to this whole horrible nightmare. But he didn't. His lips came downwards again and she tensed, bracing herself for more pain. However, this time his kiss was almost gentle, persuasively potent, changing the timbre of her response with almost indecent ease.

Carolyn's tension underwent a very subtle transition as her nerve-endings began to tingle, turning her aversion to a hungry wanting. Her hands automatically slid up, winding around his neck, her fingers threading into the thick dark strands of his hair. Leith's arms had wrapped around her, shaping her to him, making her so very aware of his own arousal, setting her aflame.

He pushed her robe from her shoulders and it fell to the floor, his fingers finding her breast, slipping beneath the thin material of her nightdress to tease one hardening peak. Carolyn moaned softly, throwing her head back so that he could nibble quick warm kisses down the curve of her throat, lower, pushing aside her nightdress, seeking the sweet valley between her breasts.

'God, it's been too long,' he murmured thickly, and she clutched him desperately to her, mindless of all else save the delirious wonder of his lovemaking.

Then they were on the bed. Somehow Leith had removed her nightdress, shed his robe, and their naked burning skin slid damply together. They moved as one, hungry for each other, like lovers who had been separated for centuries. And when their climax came Leith's mouth covered hers as she cried out his name.

When Carolyn eventually woke, opening her eyes, the light was still burning and his head was cradled on her shoulder, his body growing heavy on hers. She shifted a little and he stirred, his lips moving against the smoothness of her shoulder for short seconds. Then, as though he'd fully woken, he lifted himself from her to stretch out on his side of the bed.

A cold chill of fear gripped her in a painful grasp.

'Leith?' she ventured huskily.

'Go to sleep, Carolyn,' he said tiredly, reaching out to switch off the light.

In the darkness she turned over, away from him, drawing the sheet up to her chin, and no matter how hard she tried she couldn't stem the flow of hot tears that welled in her eyes. If Leith was aware of her distress he gave no sign, and he was asleep long before Carolyn's muffled sobs had ceased.

'Will your parents still be arriving tomorrow?' she asked him as they waited in an uneasy silence for Bodie to join them next morning.

'Yes. I'll collect them from the airport in the afternoon. We should be home by six.' He flicked a glance at his wristwatch.

Carolyn clasped her hands together behind her back. 'What . . . do they know that I . . . that Bodie doesn't . . .' She swallowed.

'They know. There'll be nothing said in front of him.'

'Thank you,' she said quietly.

'And Carolyn,' Leith's eyes turned coldly to hers, 'as far as my parents know the past is no problem between us and you and I are very happily married. I want them to go on thinking that, so I expect you to play the part in their presence.'

His whole demeanour that morning was cold and distant, as though their lovemaking those few short hours ago had never happened, was some erotic figment of her imagination. But it had happened. Pain twisted inside her and she wanted to lash out at him.

'As well as I played my part last night, behind closed doors?' she asked him bitterly.

His lips thinned angrily and she thought she saw a mometary flush colour his cheeks. 'I would have said we both got some enjoyment last night, wouldn't you?'

'How could you turn something so beautiful into a sordid, cheap——?'

'Oh, no, Carolyn, not me,' he broke in on her. 'How could *you*?'

She gazed at him powerlessly.

'Just remember what I said about not upsetting my parents,' he told her, turning away.

'Or?' she jeered defiantly, pain driving her to goad him further.

'Or, by heaven, I'll make you pay for it!' He glanced towards the door, and they both heard Bodie's footsteps approaching. 'Remember, you have so much more to lose, Carolyn.'

She simply stared at his set face in disbelief. 'You'd use Bodie to . . .? That's blackmail, Leith.'

He shrugged. 'Call it what you like. The intimacies, for want of a better word, of our marriage are no subject for discussion, not even within my family.'

The door opened and somehow Carolyn summoned a smile as her son came out on to the verandah with his bag.

'See you later, Mum.' Bodie kissed her goodbye and followed Leith over to the car. She could hear him telling Leith about some facet of his training as they both climbed into the Jaguar.

Bodie had gone to his room to change while Carolyn was checking the roast chicken she had cooked for dinner when Leith's car pulled up in the drive next evening. She took a deep steadying breath. However was she going to carry off her meeting with Leith's parents? Knowing they knew who she was was almost as bad as worrying if they'd recognise her.

Shakily she shed her apron and ran a hand over her dress. She wore a plain lemon frock and dainty white high-heeled sandals and she had fixed her hair into its chignon. Very cool and controlled—she could almost laugh at that. Car doors were closing as she walked nervously towards the front of the house.

'Are they here?' Bodie asked excitedly as he joined her, opening the door for her and stepping out on to the verandah behind her.

The sun had almost set and in the pool of light from the verandah lamp Carolyn's eyes met those of Leith's mother, eyes the same shape as Leith's but just slightly lighter in colour, and she felt her heartbeats hammering erratically against her ribcage.

Lydia McCabe moved first, walking up the steps towards Carolyn and Bodie, smilingly holding out her unbandaged hand.

'Carolyn, we meet at last! I was so annoyed with myself that I couldn't make your wedding. Falling over in that department store was such a foolish thing to do.'

Carolyn took the older woman's hand.

'I can't tell you how happy John and I were when Leith surprised us with his marriage plans. And from what he's told us about you we couldn't have asked for a nicer daughter-in-law.'

'Thank you, Mrs McCabe.' Carolyn expelled the tense breath she'd been holding.

'Please, call me Lydia, my dear.' She turned slightly. 'And this is Bodie. Suzy showed us the newspaper article written about your swimming success. You must be very proud of yourself.'

'Thanks,' grinned Bodie. 'That was the very best week of my life, winning the medals for the State team and then Mum and Leith getting engaged. It was perfect!'

Oh, Bodie, it *was* perfect. Carolyn swallowed convulsively and she turned to seek out her husband, but he gave no sign he'd heard Bodie's statement.

'Carolyn—Bodie.' Leith joined them on the verandah. 'This is my father.'

'Welcome to the family.' John McCabe stepped forward to kiss Carolyn on the cheek. 'A little late but sincere nonetheless. And to you, Bodie.'

Bodie took the older man's proffered hand.

'Let's go inside and I'll show you your room.' Leith had their suitcases and he led them into the living-room.

'Mum's cooked us a fabulous meal,' Bodie told them enthusiastically. 'Do you like roast chicken?'

'My favourite,' smiled Leith's mother.

'Mine, too,' agreed Bodie.

'And what a lovely house. Such good luck Suzy and Tim's friends were off to Canada. Now you'll be able to take your time looking for the right house.'

'If you'd like to freshen up Leith will show you your room while I put the finishing touches to dinner,' Carolyn suggested, and escaped to the kitchen, leaving Leith and Bodie to show Leith's parents to the main guest-room.

She was straightening the cutlery for the umpteenth time when she heard a sound behind her and swung around to see Leith standing in the doorway unsmilingly surveying the beautifully laid lace-covered dining-room table.

'You needn't have gone to so much trouble. I intended that we'd go out for dinner this evening.'

'It was no trouble. I like cooking, and I thought your parents might enjoy a meal at home after travelling up here.'

He walked over to her and reaching behind her untied her apron. 'So domestic, Mrs McCabe. You really are going all out to impress.'

'I'm not trying to impress anyone, not the way you mean, anyway,' she bit out angrily.

'No?' His smile was arrogantly cynical. 'There's no need anyway. You must be aware that my parents bear you no long-remembered malice. They never did blame you. Not the way I did.'

'The inquest did clear me,' she said tiredly. 'I wish you'd remember that, Leith.'

'Oh, I remember. All too well.' His hands reached out, clasping her arms, bruising the soft flesh.

Then the sound of voices coming towards the dining-room made him lift his head momentarily. With his eyes still coldly holding hers he leant forward and kissed her.

'Ah.' Lydia McCabe sighed from the doorway. 'Are we interrupting?' she chuckled delightedly.

Leith let his finger rest softly on Carolyn's lips for heart-stopping seconds before he turned to face his mother with a rueful look. 'I'm afraid I'll never become immune to those kissable lips,' he said huskily.

Carolyn dragged her eyes from his, a rosy flush colouring her cheeks. She could almost believe him! 'If you'd like to sit down I'll serve up,' she said breathlessly. 'Perhaps you could open the wine, Leith.' She fled and had to fight for composure once she reached the kitchen. How could Leith be so hard-heartedly hypocritical?

'May I help, Carolyn?' Leith's mother had followed her and Carolyn hurriedly schooled her features before she turned to face the older woman.

'I have it all ready, but you could help me carry the plates into the dining-room if you would. Can you manage with your wrist?'

'Yes. And, Carolyn,' Lydia put a gentle hand on Carolyn's arm, 'before we join the others. Leith told us you don't want the past brought up in front of your son, and I wanted to reassure you that we respect that. I can't say we weren't shocked when we discovered who you were, but the past is the past.' A flash of remembered pain crossed her face. 'At the time, that awful time, we were devastated. But the passing years have been a great salve.' She looked sadly at Carolyn. 'Anyway, we won't discuss it. I just wanted you to know John and I are simply happy that Leith has found someone he cares for so deeply. It means so much to us.'

'Thank you, Mrs . . . Lydia.' Carolyn swallowed. 'I love Leith, too, and I'll do everything in my power to make him happy.'

'I know you will.' She blinked mistily. 'Now perhaps

we'd best take the food in or they'll wonder where we are.'

'And what are you doing for Christmas?' asked Lydia the evening before they were leaving to return to Melbourne. 'Each year the family usually gets together at our place. Do you think you'll be able to join us, Leith?'

Christmas? Carolyn almost started in surprise when she realised Christmas was only a little over a week away and she hadn't even given it a thought. Usually they had decorated the house by now, and they had a tree. She glanced at Bodie.

'Gee, hasn't it come up quickly? I guess the wedding put Christmas right out of our minds.' He turned to Carolyn. 'We haven't even got a tree yet, Mum.'

'We hadn't really discussed Christmas,' Leith put in vaguely. 'That trouble in Fiji threw everything out with our plans.'

'Didn't you say you and Carolyn were planning a proper honeymoon after Christmas?' frowned his mother.

'My schedule's pretty hectic just at present,' he took a sip of his drink, 'so we've postponed our month in the Caribbean for a while.'

'Oh, that's disappointing,' sympathised Lydia.

'Why don't you let Dave handle this Fijian project so that you can get away,' suggested his father. 'There's no point in being a slave to your work, not when you have as attractive a distraction as Carolyn.' He chuckled.

'We'll have to see how it fits in with Bodie's swimming commitments,' Leith said evenly.

'After the Queensland State Open and Age Group Championships in early January I haven't got any major swims until the end of February,' Bodie told Leith, 'so that gives you and Mum plenty of time to get away for your honeymoon.'

'There you are, Leith.' John McCabe sat forward in his

seat. 'Lydia and I were thinking of spending some time at the unit on the Coast, so Bodie's quite welcome to stay with us. Suzy's bringing the girls up, too. And I'm sure between Dave, Tim and myself we can see to your business interests.' He smiled and rubbed his hands together. 'In fact, I'd enjoy a few weeks back at the helm.'

'I'll see how things go.' Leith finished his drink in one gulp, and Carolyn could almost sympathise with him. He obviously had no desire whatsoever to spend any time with her and he was going to get out of it any way he could.

'And do you think you'll all make it down to Melbourne for Christmas?' his mother persisted.

'I guess so,' Leith conceded. 'But I'll be tied up pretty well until Christmas Eve. We'll fly down in the afternoon in the company jet.'

'Wow!' ejaculated Bodie, round-eyed.

'Lovely,' beamed Lydia. 'Dave will be back from the States, too, so the whole family will be together. Won't that be perfect?'

Perfect, Carolyn thought bitterly, and then felt dreadfully guilty. As a mother Lydia had every right to be happy her family would be gathered around her. This terrible dissension between herself and Leith had nothing to do with his mother, so it was hardly her fault. In fact Leith's parents had been marvellous about the whole thing when they could so easily have been exactly the opposite.

If Carolyn was honest with herself she would have to admit that most of her tension stemmed from the fact that Leith's parents were leaving the next day. At least while they were here she could almost believe Leith still loved her.

Except when they were alone together, something he made sure they rarely were. Since the night they'd made love he hadn't so much as touched her, even as they lay in the huge double bed.

Dark circles appeared under Carolyn's eyes as she spent night after night lying sleeplessly beside him feeling desperately alone.

She got up to make some coffee and her mother-in-law joined her. 'I do hope having us here hasn't been too tiring for you, my dear,' she frowned, looking at Carolyn's pale face.

'Oh, no, of course it hasn't,' Carolyn reassured her. 'I've loved meeting you and having you with us. I just wish you could stay longer.'

'I do, too, Carolyn. But we promised Suzy's elder daughter we'd be back for her birthday, so we must go. I really don't know how we managed before John retired. We seem to lead such a busy life.' Her eyes searched Carolyn's face. 'Try to talk Leith into going away after Christmas. He's been working far too hard and needs a break, too. In fact I'm sure a few weeks on your own would do wonders for both of you.'

They were just about to leave for the airport next day when the phone rang. Carolyn raced back into the house and picked up the receiver.

'Carolyn.' Leith's deep voice had its familiar effect on her. 'I'm glad I caught you, I need some papers urgently and I haven't time to come out to the house to collect them. Do you mind dropping them here at the office after you've taken Mum and Dad to the airport?'

'No, of course not. Where are they?'

'It's the file on the Edward Street site, in the top drawer of my desk.'

'I'll just make sure I can find it.' Carolyn hurried into Leith's study and returned with the file. 'I have it here. But I'll be at least an hour, unless you want me to drop the file off on the way to the airport.'

'No, that would be too much of a rush. Besides, I won't be back at the office until four. I'm seeing one of the subcontractors about four-thirty.' He paused. 'I'll see you later, then.' The line went dead and Carolyn slowly replaced the receiver and left the house.

She dropped Bodie off at training and then continued out to the airport with Leith's parents. Now, as she turned into the familiar car park beneath Kruger's she could almost believe she was still working there. Apart, that was, from her expensive new clothes and the quietly purring impeccably behaved BMW.

She stepped into the lift and as it soared upwards she caught sight of her reflection in the shiny surface of the cubicle's wall. In her white linen suit, the straight skirt split up one side to mid-thigh showing off her long nylon-clad legs, and the short-sleeved tailored jacket worn over a pastel-blue blouse that brought out the blue-grey in her smoky eyes she could have stepped from the pages of a fashion magazine. Her fair hair, professionally styled now, swung loosely to her shoulders and she knew her make-up was flawless.

A woman who has everything. Carolyn could see the words splashed across the glossy page of the magazine and her lips twisted bitterly. Everything. Yes, she had everything. Everything except the thing she most wanted: Leith's love. But that had gone, too, had become part of yesterday.

The lift stopped and she stepped out into the hallway, turning instinctively towards her office. Tapping on the door, she forced a smile on to her face and went inside, ready to show Maggie everything in her garden was rosy. But the room was empty.

Slowly she crossed to the connecting door, but there was no answer to her tentative knock, so she opened the door and went into her husband's office. It was as neat and austere as it always was and she placed the folder he had wanted in the middle of his desk. With an involuntary sigh she returned to Maggie's office just as the door opened and Trevor came in with a pile of papers under his arm.

'Carolyn!' His eyes lit up, his gaze roving over her. 'Nice to see you.'

'How are you, Trevor?'

'Fine. I'll just give these papers to Leith and we'll have a chat.'

'Leith's not in yet.'

'Oh.' Trevor glanced at his watch and then indicated the coffee-machine. 'Have you time for a cup of coffee?'

'I'd love one, but let me get it.' She poured two cups while Trevor put his papers down on Maggie's desk.

'Maggie's having the afternoon off,' he told her as she passed him his coffee and he took a sip. 'Marriage suits you,' he said with a crooked smile. 'You look beautiful.'

'Thank you, Trevor.' Carolyn inclined her head but didn't meet his eyes.

'And have you decided to stay in Brisbane?' He spoke into the small silence.

'We haven't had time to discuss it yet. Things have been hectic these past weeks.'

Trevor nodded and made a sweeping gesture of the office. 'Well, do you miss all this?'

'Not yet.' She smiled and leant back against the desk. As she did so some of Trevor's papers slid to the floor and they both went down on their haunches to pick them up.

'I'm sorry, Trevor,' Carolyn apologised.

'No damage done.' He took the papers from her and they slowly stood up.

They were standing close together and he frowned, putting his hand out towards her. 'Carolyn——'

Whatever he had been about to say was left unsaid as the door opened and they both swung around.

Leith's tall broad frame filled the doorway as he paused there, his eyes going coldly from Trevor to Carolyn before he slowly closed the door behind him and strolled lithely forward. Trevor dropped his hand and stepped quickly away.

'Sorry I'm late, darling.' Leith's arm went possessively

around Carolyn's shoulder and his lips touched her cheek. 'Have you been waiting long?'

'No, not long.' She almost flinched as his fingers slid down her arm, encircling her wrist, tightening painfully. She tried to pull away but he held her fast. 'The file you wanted is on your desk,' she said as levelly as she could manage.

'Thanks.' He turned to Trevor. 'And what about those estimates I asked for?'

Trevor started forward. 'I have them here.' He handed Leith the pile of papers.

'Good. Well, don't let us keep you,' said Leith with barely a shred of civility.

'No. I do have a lot more work to get through, so if you'll excuse me I'll see you both later.' He darted a glance at Carolyn and left them.

Carolyn took a steadying breath as she fought to suppress her anger. 'I should be going, too. I want to be home when Joy drops Bodie off,' she managed evenly enough.

'That won't be for a couple of hours yet,' Leith frowned.

'I might do a little shopping before I leave the city—some jeans for Bodie.' Her voice faded away as his fingers tightened again.

'Don't think I'll stand idly by and watch you make doe-eyes at Green,' he said icily, and she stared up at him.

'Make——? Don't be ridiculous. We'd only been talking for a few minutes when you walked in!' she gasped angrily.

Leith gave a cynical laugh. 'It looked very cosy from where I stood.'

Carolyn shook her head. 'I don't have to stay here and listen to this, Leith. Please let go of my arm, I want to go home.'

'But that's not what I want, Carolyn.' His voice dropped huskily and he pulled her against his hard body, his lips lowering to cover hers with no vestige of tenderness.

She pushed her hands against his chest, but she was no match for his superior strength. He held one arm trapped behind her and when he finally released her mouth her eyes flashed her anger at him.

'Let me go, Leith. I can't bear you to touch me.'

'Can't you, Carolyn?' He smiled mockingly. 'Your body tells me a very different story.'

She struggled against him, but he held her with easy arrogance. 'Why, you——! Let me go!' she bit out. 'Unless you intend adding rape to your manly virtues,' she jeered, and he stilled, his head lifting, his eyes blazing.

'Rape, Carolyn?' He gave a harsh laugh as he slowly let her go. 'Don't delude yourself. I wouldn't need to rape you and we both know it, don't we?'

Carolyn drew a steadying breath. 'I'm going back to the house and I'm packing our things. I really can't see any point in continuing this farce.' She started for the door.

'Carolyn, I told you you're my wife and you'll stay my wife until I decide to change that.' He grabbed her arm again, spinning her back to face him.

The knock on the door held them silently motionless for immeasurable seconds before Leith reluctantly released her arm and moved away from her.

'Come in,' he called curtly.

The door opened and one of their subcontractors walked into the office. 'Afternoon, Leith, Mrs All . . ., that is, Mrs McCabe,' he corrected quickly.

'Hello, Tom.' Carolyn forced a smile. 'I'll leave you and Leith to your discussion,' she finished hurriedly, and almost bolted from the room.

Once she reached the sanctuary of the house she went straight to her room and lifted out her new suitcase, throwing it on the bed. But then the anger seemed to drain out of her and she sank on to the soft spread and brushed her suddenly tear-filled eyes with her hand. What was she going to do? She twisted her glittering gold wedding-ring as tears cascaded unchecked down her cheeks. Oh, Leith, why did it have to end so soon? If only . . .

When a car door closed she wiped at her wet face and started towards the bedroom door. Now that Bodie was here she'd have to try to explain to him why they had to leave.

'I'm in here, love,' she called to him as she opened the door. But it wasn't Bodie who strode down the hallway towards her, it was Leith, and his set expression had her stepping backwards into the bedroom.

Leith followed her and his eyes took in the suitcase on the bed. In one stride he had scooped it up and thrown it violently back into the closet. Then he turned angrily back to her.

'Oh, no! I said you were staying and, by God, you'll stay, even if I have to lock you in this room!'

'You can't do that,' Carolyn got out, fear clutching at her as his icy anger reached out to enmesh her in paralysing tentacles.

'Can't I? Just try me.'

Her hand went nervously to her throat. 'Leith, please, we can't go on like this.' She felt her shoulders sag tiredly. 'What happened to us?'

'You can ask that?' he threw at her. 'I found out what a lying little bitch you were, that's what happened!'

'I never lied to you. For heaven's sake, surely you can understand why I didn't tell you who I was?' Her voice broke. 'What do you want of me, Leith? Do I have to keep paying for loving you too much to risk losing you?' She looked levelly at him. 'Because I did love you, more than I can tell you.'

His eyes impaled her coldly. 'More than you loved Bodie's father?'

Carolyn held his gaze. 'Yes, more than I loved Bodie's father,' she said softly.

His anger seemed to intensify. 'Where's Bodie's birth certificate?' he asked harshly, and she frowned in surprise.

'Why . . . why would you want that?'

'All this talk of love,' he sneered, and in two strides he was on her, his hands dragging her forward, hard against his taut body. 'Love had nothing to do with why you married me, did it, Carolyn? You married me for some perverted form of revenge!'

'What are you talking about?' Carolyn's voice rose thinly.

'You were playing one off against the other all those years ago, weren't you? Now, no more games, Carolyn. I have to know. Is Bodie my nephew?'

For numbing seconds Carolyn couldn't comprehend his meaning, and when the implications of his question dawned on her she began to shake her head.

'Is he, Carolyn? Answer me!' He shook her brutally. 'Was Chris his father?'

A cold anger that more than matched his own rose inside her and she knew an almost overwhelming urge to flay him with her nails. That anger gave her strength and she tore herself out of his grip.

'My God, how can you ask that?' She held up her hand as he went to move towards her again. 'No. No, let me guess. The great Leith McCabe can't bear the thought of having his brother's left-over. Isn't that it?'

'Carolyn!' he warned.

She gave a mirthless laugh. 'You egotistical, arrogant——'

He reached for her again. 'Don't I have a right to know?' he ground out.

'Right? What right? You professed to love me enough to make me your wife and accept Bodie into your family.' She gazed defiantly up at him. 'Well, you'll never know,

Leith, because there's no father's name on Bodie's birth certificate. His father never lived to sign the forms.'

'Carolyn, I——'

'Mum—Leith. What's going on? Why are you yelling?' Bodie dropped his bag and came towards them, his young face troubled. His eyes took in Leith's hands biting into Carolyn's arms and he paused, his expression growing suddenly very adult. 'Let Mum go, Leith,' he said quietly. 'Let her go.'

Their eyes locked and Bodie's barely flickered. After a moment Leith dropped his hands, setting Carolyn free.

'Why are you fighting?' Bodie's gaze shifted to his mother.

'Bodie,' Carolyn started forward, 'I didn't realise the time.' She put her arm around him and for the first time he stood stiffly in her grasp.

'You were fighting about me, weren't you?' he said flatly.

'Oh, love, we weren't. Not really. It was nothing to do with you,' she tried to reassure him.

Bodie's questioning eyes went from Leith back to his mother. 'Did you know Leith before? I mean, before he came to Kruger's?'

Carolyn swallowed. 'I——' She couldn't lie to him. But what could she say?

'Your mother and I met fourteen years ago, before you were born,' Leith told him flatly.

Bodie took this in and Carolyn could see him considering Leith's answer as he turned to look straight at her.

'Bodie——' she began, but his gaze had returned to Leith.

'Are you my father?' he asked levelly.

CHAPTER ELEVEN

CAROLYN'S breath caught in her throat and Leith's face had paled. Her arm tightened instinctively about her son and he looked back at her.

'Is he my father?'

'No, Bodie, he isn't,' she answered him. 'I've never lied to you about that. Your father was killed six months before you were born.'

'Then why——?' Bodie swallowed.

'Leith and I . . . There were things I hadn't told Leith, about my life before you were born, and——'

'What does that matter?' Bodie turned to Leith, angry now, struggling for control. 'If you really love someone what they did before shouldn't matter at all. Mum's never told me, but I worked it out she wasn't married to my father—but that doesn't mean she was bad. I can tell you she's always been the best mother anyone could ever have, and . . . and I love her.' He drew a tortured breath. 'And I won't let anyone say anything against her, not even you, Leith. So if you don't love her then you can go. We don't need you.' His voice cracked and he bit his trembling lip as he hurried out of the room.

Carolyn went to follow him, but Leith's hand on her arm stopped her. 'Leave him, Carolyn,' he said softly, his anger gone, but she shook off his touch.

'Bodie's right, Leith. I thought I wanted you on any terms, but he's right. We don't need you. I protested my innocence at that inquest years ago and I'm tired of having to keep protesting it to you now. I think you'd better go.' With that she left him, and she heard the door close behind him as she went into Bodie's room. And she refused to admit that part of her still cried out for Leith to stay.

The alarm dragged her from a fitful sleep next morning and she struggled out of bed. Slipping on her robe, she deliberately turned away from the empty bed and went to wake Bodie. She'd spent ages with him after Leith left, explaining everything to him, telling him the whole story.

'I don't think I'll go to training today,' he said, making no attempt to get up, not looking at her.

'But you've never missed a day's training.' Carolyn sat down on the side of his bed.

'Will we be leaving today?' He kept his eyes on the ceiling.

'I suppose so. There are people in our flat for the next six months, so we'll have to find somewhere to stay until their lease expires.'

Bodie sighed and turned to face her. 'Do you think he'll come back?' he asked quietly.

Carolyn shook her head. 'I don't know, love.'

'I'm sorry, Mum, that it's turned out this way.'

She nodded and stood up.

Bodie got out of bed. 'I really did think he was—well, I thought he was okay.' He put his arms around her and Carolyn rested her weary head against his.

'I did, too, love. I did, too.'

They were drinking a cup of tea when the key turned in the front door and Leith walked in. Carolyn clutched the breakfast-bar for support and she felt Bodie move beside her.

Leith looked haggard. He obviously hadn't slept and he badly needed a shave. His eyes met Carolyn's and she saw a flash of pain in them before he came forward glancing at his watch.

'No training this morning, Bodie?' he asked.

'I—er—was going to give it a miss,' Bodie replied quietly.

'How about I drive you? I'd like to talk to you. And your mother and I have a lot to discuss, too.'

Bodie hesitated and Leith gave him a crooked smile. 'No rough stuff—I give you my word.'

Bodie glanced at Carolyn and she nodded. 'Okay, I'll get my bag.' He left them together.

Carolyn's heartbeats were skipping over themselves. She longed to reach out, touch him, smooth the lines from his drawn face.

'Would you like some tea?' she asked huskily.

'Please.'

He drank it down as Bodie reappeared. After a moment's uncertainty Bodie followed Leith out to the car.

As they drove away Carolyn was stirred into action. She hurriedly showered and slipped into a plain green skirt and a loose apple-green blouse. With shaky hands she applied a little make-up to her pale face and the dark cirles under her eyes. She was brushing her hair when Leith returned. Dared she hope——?

He stopped in the doorway and tiredly rubbed his chin. 'We need to talk, Carolyn,' he said flatly. 'But I'd like to shower first. Do you mind?'

She shook her head and for heart-stopping seconds he held her gaze, his face expressionless. Then he continued on to the bathroom. By the time he returned to find her in the living-room Carolyn's stomach was churning and her whole body was painfully tense. He was wearing clean scrub denims and a light towelling shirt and she could smell the tang of his spicy aftershave mingled with the soap he had used, his hair still damp. How she yearned to throw herself into his arms, to beg him to forgive her. Her eyes rose to meet his and she saw her own pain reflected there.

'Forgive me,' he said huskily, and Carolyn was too stunned to speak. 'Although God knows I don't deserve it. My only excuse is that I was so consumed by jealousy I couldn't think straight. I must have been a little mad. I couldn't see past the thought of you and Chris——'

He stopped and ran an unsteady hand over his eyes. 'It wasn't that you hadn't told me who you were. It wasn't even the thought of another unknown man making love to you. But when I thought Bodie's father was Chris, my own brother, I . . .' He drew a shaky breath. 'As you said, I had no right. No right at all. I'm not proud of myself, Carolyn. Less so for selfishly allowing Bodie to be upset the way he was last night.'

Carolyn could see the regret in his eyes.

'After I left all I could think about as I drove around was you and Chris together. Then something hit me so hard I reeled, something Bodie said. When you love someone you don't question their past. You asked nothing of mine, and I'm far from being a saint.' He grimaced self-derisively. 'By then I was hours away and I broke all the speed limits getting back. I was so afraid my stupid blind jealousy had lost me the one thing that meant more to me than life itself. You.' His eyes held hers. 'Has it, Caro?'

Carolyn took a faltering step towards him, tears running down her cheeks. 'Oh, Leith!' she whispered, and he met her halfway. She wound her arms around his neck, sliding quick kisses along his jawline, over his cheek. 'You could never lose me. You'll have to send me away.'

'God, Caro!' He clasped her to him, his face buried in the softness of her hair. 'It would be like cutting out my heart,' he said thickly, and then they were kissing, deep, hungry, desperate kisses.

Finally Leith led her over to a comfy chair and pulled her down on to his lap. He smiled tenderly at her. 'I'm almost afraid to believe you're here, close to me.'

Carolyn ran her finger gently down his cheek. 'I really am sorry I didn't tell you I was Carol Barton. When you didn't recognise me I . . . You see I thought you'd simply sort out the office at Kruger's and then move on. And later, when I realised I was in love with you, I was afraid to tell you.'

His fingers covered her hand. 'When Chris was killed, it was a bad time for the family. I probably didn't recognise you because I literally blacked out those weeks. I had to.' He sighed. 'When I hit out at you all those years ago I was really attacking myself. I was being eaten away by my own guilt.'

She raised her eyebrows. 'But you had nothing whatsoever to do with it.'

'I was responsible for Chris having that motor-cycle. Our parents refused to let him buy it at first, but he talked me into helping him change their minds. He was my young brother and I well—I'd been through that stage myself and come out unscathed. I knew he had to get it out of his system. I arranged for him to have lessons so that he could handle the machine and I talked Mum and Dad around.'

'Leith, you couldn't have known it would end the way it did,' Carolyn told him.

'Maybe not. But Chris was the youngest, Mum's favourite, and I blamed myself. That's the real reason I blew my cool at the inquest. I shouldn't have treated you the way I did. Not then and not now.'

She shook her head. 'I've carried the same guilt with me, too, that I should have stopped the fight somehow. But it was just a chain of events that no one could change. I couldn't know Terry and Chris would fight over me and Chris couldn't see that Terry would hit his head on the kerb.' She looked at him earnestly. 'But there was never anything between Chris and me. Please believe that. I only ever—there was only Terry.'

'I should have listened to my parents.' Leith expelled a tortured breath. 'Back then my father tried to tell me you were the innocent party caught up in it all. I remember he called you a troubled child. He said Chris's time had come, that fate was to blame, no one and nothing else

When he told me on the phone that he recognised you I——' He shook his head. 'It was lucky he couldn't see my face. He thought I knew and I was too shocked to set him straight. And then anger took over—blind, irrational, jealous anger. It was as though I were standing watching myself, totally horrified, but unable to do a thing about my actions.' He lifted a strand of her hair and watched it slide silkily through his fingers. 'Can you forgive me, Caro? Can we go on from here, leave the past behind us where it belongs?' He looked deeply into her eyes. 'I love you, Carolyn, more than I'd have believed I could love anyone. And I don't want to lose you.'

'I love you too, Leith.' She raised her lips to his and they kissed, gently at first, feeling the passion rising between them.

'Mmm what you do to me!' Leith groaned. 'What you've always done to me!'

'Increased your need for cold showers?' Carolyn chuckled teasingly.

'They never worked,' he grimaced self-derisively, 'as I proved the night before my parents arrived. I tried to stay away from you, but so help me, I couldn't. I had to feel you in my arms again.' He gave a soft laugh, and ran his hand lingeringly down her backbone, making her shiver delightedly. 'It's been like that since the moment I saw you, when you fell at my feet.'

'I had the shock of my life when you opened the door. I couldn't believe it was actually you.'

'But you did fall at my feet, Mrs McCabe.'

Carolyn laughed. 'I did, didn't I?' She softly followed the line of his nose with her finger, stopping at his lips. 'Were you really attracted to me from the very first moment?' she asked him.

Leith nodded. 'I felt as if I'd been king-hit. And it had never happened to me before. I was always in control, I set the pace in a relationship. But,' he shrugged, 'you didn't exactly give me the impression you were interested. Quite the reverse. Why do you think I was such a slave-driver in the office?'

'You were, weren't you?'

'Then there was Green hanging around hopefully.'

'Oh, Leith, there was nothing between Trevor and me,' Carolyn told him.

'I still could have torn him limb from limb. Can I plead insanity due to dead green jealousy?' He lifted her blouse from the waist of her skirt and his fingers teased her bare skin. 'I don't know how I kept my hands off you all those weeks.'

'And I never even thought about—well, sex, before you came along,' she admitted. 'Then I couldn't seem to get it off my mind.'

'Ah!' Leith nibbled her earlobe. 'And is it on your mind now?'

'You just might be able to jog my memory. Perhaps I need a little prompting, hmm?' She ran her lips along the line of his jaw.

'You realise it will put *that look* back on your face, Mrs McCabe?'

'*That look*, Mr McCabe?' Carolyn feigned innocence.

'The look of a woman who's just made love. The look you didn't want Bodie to see.' His lips nibbled hers.

'Leith.' Carolyn sat up. 'Bodie will be back from training——'

'I said we'd pick him up.' Leith glanced at his watch 'He won't mind if we're a little late. I made my peace with him, I think, once I'd told him I intended to beg your forgiveness. He's something else, Carolyn. Just like his beautiful mother.' He kissed her almost reverently.

'Mmm,' Carolyn murmured and moved sensuously against him. 'You know, I really think Bodie will need reassuring that everything's all right between us again. Do you suppose if I had *that look* it might help?' Her fingertip traced the outline of his lips.

Leith stood up, lifting her in his arms. 'I think it would help enormously,' he agreed, his eyes full of burning promise. 'Besides, Bodie's not the only one who needs to be reassured,' he whispered throatily as he carried her along the hall to their bedroom.